the

GREAT

Christmas

BOWL

the
GREAT
Christmas
BOWL

a Christmas novella

SUSAN MAY WARREN

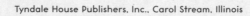

Tyndale House Publishers, Inc., Carol Stream, Illinois

Visit Tyndale's exciting Web site at www.tyndale.com

Visit Susan May Warren's Web site at www.susanmaywarren.com

TYNDALE and Tyndale's quill logo are registered trademarks of Tyndale House Publishers, Inc.

The Great Christmas Bowl

Designed by Jessie McGrath

Edited by Sarah Mason

Scripture taken from the HOLY BIBLE, NEW INTERNATIONAL VERSION®. NIV®. Copyright © 1973, 1978, 1984 by International Bible Society. Used by permission of Zondervan. All rights reserved.

Library of Congress Cataloging-in-Publication Data

Warren, Susan May, date.
　The great Christmas bowl / Susan May Warren.
　　p. cm.
　ISBN 978-1-4143-2678-8
　1. Christmas stories.　I. Title.
　PS3623.A865G74 2009
　813'.6—dc22　　　　　　　　　　　　　　　　2009005470

Printed in the United States of America

15　14　13　12　11　10　09
　7　6　5　4　3　2　1

For my precious family:

Andrew, David, Sarah, Peter, and Noah.

A NOTE FROM THE AUTHOR

I love football. And I love Christmas. And I love being a mother.

Last year, two monumental occurrences happened in the Warren life. First, my son Peter went out for football. I went berserk with joy and became a little over-the-top obsessed with supporting him. (So maybe he doesn't need brownies before *every* game.) I created my own cheering section. I was the loud mom in the bleachers. I realized about halfway through the season that football had created a monster out of me. (It wasn't all my fault—he kept scoring touchdowns!)

About the same time, my oldest son, David, got the lead in the community play—as Daddy Warbucks in *Annie*. On opening night, he came out on stage, head shaved, shoulders broad in a tuxedo, singing in his rich tenor, and I burst into tears that would last the entire Christmas season as I realized next year he'd be heading off to college. It didn't help that my beautiful daughter, Sarah, got the role of Lily St. Regis, and when she opened her mouth to sing, I hardly recognized the grown woman onstage. Even Noah, my youngest, amazed me as he sang in the cast, and I wondered where my babies had gone.

Obviously, *The Great Christmas Bowl* was already simmering deep in my heart. But it never would have found the light of day if it hadn't been for Rachel Hauck. While attending our friend Anne's wedding in Nashville, we spent one evening watching college football and dreamed up a fun story about an obsessive mother during football season. (At the time, I might have had a lot of church activities on my plate, also.) We each had our own vision for the story and pledged that the first one who wrote it got to keep the idea. I went straight home and opened my computer.

But I was stuck on the mascot. I envisioned a beaver. Or a moose. But they didn't quite fit. So I asked the plotting mastermind who lives with me—my husband, Andrew. He shrugged and said, "Of course, it's a trout." Of *course*. And the Big Lake Trout was born.

I wrote this story over the Christmas season like a tailback, head down, plowing through the defensive line, my eyes on the end zone. I laughed aloud. I cried (I still do when I read the end). And my children gave me the biggest gift of all for Christmas—they let me read it aloud to them at the dinner table every night. And *they* laughed. And they told me they loved it.

As a test, to see if I wasn't just dreaming up my own humor (maybe I still am), I gave it to my pal Ellen Tarver, who read it and, once again, helped me tweak it so it was just right.

I wrote the *Bowl* as a gift for my family. Because, you see, it's us. We have clam chowder (see recipe in the back). We have the Great Christmas Tree Hunt in the backyard, we have the crazy dog Gracie, and we live in a magical small town that may or may not look like the fictional Big Lake, with an amazing, loving church family (who resemble none of the players in the story, I might add!). Most of all, we love Christmas and our traditions.

I never thought the *Bowl* would really be published, so I'm grateful to my agent, Steve Laube, for loving the book and showing it to Karen Watson, who encouraged me by also loving it. And to Tyndale, for believing in the story, as simple and crazy as it is, and to Sarah Mason, who smoothed out all the rough edges.

Most of all, I'm grateful to God, who plunked this story in my heart and gave me a rich life, an incredible family, and the gift of salvation. I'm so grateful that He reached out of heaven to the downtrodden, the lost, and the hungry people who didn't know Him, to give us eternal nourishment so we will hunger no more. This, I believe, is the true meaning of hospitality. I pray this Christmas season, you see the hospitality of Jesus Christ in your life.

Merry Christmas!
Susan May Warren

PROLOGUE

THERE ARE SOME Christmases that slink by, their significance lost amid the flurry of parties, holiday card mailings, and the endless lists of stocking stuffers. They end well, perhaps, with a sigh of relief and a warm curl of happiness that signifies, once again, a successful season had by all.

There are other years, however, that stand out in stark relief. Moments when the trudge of time, however briefly, hiccups. Years when we remember exactly why we gather with family to celebrate a day of peace, of grace.

For me, such a stumble in time came in my forty-eighth year. The year I turned into a fish.

It happened by accident, as all monumental occurrences do. In fact, it wasn't until afterward that I realized the depth of what had transpired. My youngest son claims that I entered into my state fully cognizant of the ramifications. My perspective suggests I was tricked, baited by the hope that my youngest son might find inspiration and purpose in my humble transformation and sacrifice.

Perhaps he did. But that year, the year I became a fish, also turned out to be the Christmas that would remind me, in years hence, that children do remember. They hold the memories we create as nourishment, filling in the nooks and crannies of their lives to make them stronger.

And eventually, they pass them on.

"Hey, Mom, I think it's a day for soup."

The voice of said youngest son, Kevin, greets me now as he stomps into the foyer after building a snowman and takes me back for a moment to those childhood days when he'd drop his football gear with a noisy thump, kick off his boots, and trumpet into the house.

I can hardly believe he is in graduate school. Especially since I didn't think he'd graduate from high school. But here he is, home for Thanksgiving, his hair wild and long, his shoulders broader, his countenance stronger. He finally towers over his two older brothers and his sisters, of course, but he still bears that boyish smile that could make me say yes to anything.

He's the only one home this year. Of my five children, only a few sprinkle back to the homestead for Thanksgiving, their own families and in-laws commandeering their time. I don't blame them—with Big Lake located three hours north of the Twin Cities of Minneapolis and Saint Paul, smack-dab in the woodsy middle of Minnesota, who knows when a three-day blizzard might strand them for a week or more in our little lakeside town. Indeed, only two days ago, a northern preseason blizzard that I feared would keep Kevin imprisoned in the big city ushered in high hopes of a white Christmas, giving a sheen of diamonds to the shaggy black pine trees ringing our yard. The pond out back finally froze over, and trees creaked in the cold wind off the lake. Our little town will soon be decked out with ribbons and wreaths, Main Street alive with twinkle lights, the shopwindows spray-painted with holly. Normally, I would eagerly wave good-bye to the dying brown grasses of fall, stiff with cold that begged for a snowy white blanket.

However, when the weatherman predicted snow for Thanksgiving, I bemoaned the timing and stared out the window into the blackness, not at all charmed by the Rockwellian nostalgia of a holiday blizzard as I waited for my youngest son's headlights to reach up our long gravel drive.

He arrived with fanfare Wednesday night, right behind a plow, dragging with him into our icy paradise Marci, the girl he brought home for our approval. Another jolt of reality. Now she enters the house right behind him, snowy and cold, clapping off the clinging ice from her knitted mittens.

"Mrs. Wallace, Kev tells me you have the most amazing chowder." Marci peels off her scarf and glances at my son, her eyes shining.

"I thought we agreed you'd call me Marianne." I hand her a mug of hot cocoa. It's a store-bought mix, but I've relaxed my standards over the years.

Not about soup, of course.

"She has amazing soup. Miracle soup." It's then Kevin meets my eye. He's wearing that smile. "Tell her about the Great Christmas Bowl, Mom."

"Oh, Kevin, no." But even as I say it, I'm taking out the old recipe, a sudden hankering guiding my hands. I'll just whip up a quick batch, add a chunk of French bread on the side.

Kevin notices, and his blue eyes fill with laughter. "Please. It's a family story that Marci has to know. It's time, don't you think?"

No, I don't think. "I can't believe you remember that."

He shakes his head, silently saying, *Really, Mom, are you serious?* Then he leans over and lands me one of those kisses that tells me no, he'll never forget.

Truthfully, neither will I.

And as he grabs a knife to peel potatoes, I realize he still has the power to make me do anything.

Really, I mean anything.

CHAPTER

1

I'VE ALWAYS BEEN a football fan, the kind of woman who could easily find herself parked on the sofa any given Sunday afternoon, rooting for my favorite team. I've never been a gambler, never played fantasy football, never followed my team during the hot summer months. I'm a fall-season-until-Super-Bowl-only fan, but die-hard nonetheless. Something about investing my emotions for three hours in the fate of eleven men dressed in purple tights soothes my busy spirit.

Having given birth to three sons, I dreamed I'd have the makings of a starring offensive lineup. My oldest son, Neil, would play quarterback; Brett would be a running back; and my youngest, Kevin, would be a wide receiver. My daughters and I would lead cheers from the stands. My husband, Mike, who had played in our hometown high school and helped bring them to state in his senior year, would help coach. We'd be a football family, training with weights and running in the off-season. We'd plan our vacations around summer practices, and I'd join the booster club, maybe sell raffle tickets, even host the end-of-the-year potluck.

If girls could have played football in our tiny town, I know that Brianna and Amy would have joined the team. They became my cohorts, huddling under stadium blankets and clapping their mittens together as we cheered our high school team to victory.

Alas, Neil joined chess club, and Brett became a lead in the school plays.

The football gene seemed to have eluded even our youngest son. A boy who would rather sit on the sofa moving his thumbs in furious online game playing as his only form of exercise, Kevin didn't possess even a hint of interest in football. I knew he'd inherited some athleticism, as evidenced by the discarded sports equipment left in his wake over the years: hockey skates, pads, helmet, basketball shoes, a tennis racket, a baseball glove. All abandoned after one season of hopeful use.

The only sport that seemed to take had been soccer. For three years I entered into the world of soccer mom, investing in my own foldout chair and a cooler. Perhaps it was his boundless energy that allowed him to play nearly the entire game, but Kevin had a knack for getting the ball in the net. Too bad our community soccer program ended at sixth grade, because Big Lake might have had its very own star. I'd hoped his interest would transfer to football, the other fall sport, but the old pigskin seemed as interesting to Kevin as cleaning his room.

Meanwhile, Neil, Brett, Brianna, and Amy graduated and moved out of the house, bound for college—most obtaining scholarships, much to the relief of my overworked, underpaid EMT husband. By the time Kevin moved into Neil's basement teen hangout room, Neil was married and working as a CPA in Milwaukee, Brett was doing commercials in Chicago, Brianna had started graduate school for psychology, and Amy was studying abroad in London.

I worried for Kevin as he approached his senior year, envisioning him taking on a post–high school job at the local Dairy Queen while he honed his gaming skills, waiting for his future to somehow find him in the dark recesses of our basement amid his piled dirty clothing, his unmade bed, and the debris of pizza cartons. How I longed for him to grow up.

So the day he came home from school clutching a medical release form for football in his hand, I wondered if perhaps he had a high fever and needed immediate hospitalization.

"I've been thinking of playing for a while," he said, shrugging. "It's my last chance."

Summertime had begun its slide into fall, the northern nights cooling. In two short months, we'd have our first snowfall. As I stared at my son—his stringy blond hair, his muscles that just needed toning, the way his gaze slid away from me and onto the floor—I wondered if he expected me to say no.

I took the pen and signed the form without reading it.

Teenage sons are often difficult to encourage. Instead of erupting into a wild jig of joy in the middle of the kitchen, I took the subtle route. I purchased football cleats and set them by the door to his room. I filled his water bottle every morning, packing it with ice, then slipping it into his backpack. I started baking pot roasts and cutting him the largest piece. I bought Bengay, put it on his pillow. I set vitamins out for him at breakfast.

And sometimes, yes, I snuck up in my SUV and sat at the edge of the field, behind the goalposts, watching practice.

My son had talent. A lot of talent. And I wasn't the only one who noticed. Our residence in a small town played to Kevin's odds, and being bigger and faster than most of his teammates made up for his inability to block. Coach Grant started him at tackle, then moved him to fullback, then, after noting his ability to twist out of a hold (thanks to years of wrestling for the remote control with his brothers), landed him at tailback.

To my silent glee, my son had the moves of Walter

Payton and could dance his way up the field, leaping opponents, breaking tackles, and generally restoring my faith in the Wallace family football gene. I couldn't wait for the season to start. Finally, I had a Big Lake Trout.

I purchased a season pass. A stadium cushion. A foam finger.

I was the first one in the gates on the day of the season opener. Mike stood on the sidelines next to the requisite ambulance, something that I'd always noted but never fully appreciated until now.

He waved to me as I plopped down my cushion, pulled my red and black stadium blanket over my knees, and wrestled out my digital camera, prepared to capture every moment of my son's magnificent run to victory. Mike had taken Kevin out for dinner the night before for what I hoped would be a pep talk/strategic-planning session. I wasn't the only one holding tightly to silent hopes.

"You're here early."

I looked up from reviewing shots of Brianna's college graduation to see Bud Finlaysen greeting me from the field. Bundled in orange hunting coveralls as an undergarment, he wore over the top the shiny black and silver costume of the Big Lake Trout team mascot. Bud had served as the Trout since what I assumed was the dawn of time, or at least the game of football, and we needed him like summer needs lemonade. He and his fish costume comprised the entirety of our cheerleading squad. Our cheerleaders had defected three years prior, and despite the efforts of our paltry pep band, we were woefully lacking in sideline team spirit.

Bud held his headpiece under one arm, the gargantuan mouth gaping open. When worn, his face showed through the open mouth, the enormous fishy eyes googling out from atop his head, a spiky dorsal fin running along his back. He'd shove his hands into two front fins that sparkled with shiny silver material. The costume split at the bottom for his black boots, and a tail dragged behind him like a medieval dragon. Once fitted together, the Big Lake Trout towered nearly eight feet tall, although with the tail, it easily measured over ten. Ten feet of aquatic terror.

"I have a son playing tailback," I said, holding up my camera and taking a shot of Bud. "Gotta get a good seat."

Bud laughed. I remembered him from the days when I attended Big Lake High. He worked as the school janitor. Even then he seemed ancient, although he must have been only twenty years or so older than I was. Thin, with kind blue eyes and a hunch in his back, he'd drag his yellow mop bucket around the halls singing Christmas carols, even in May.

"Maybe this will be the year they go to state," he said, pulling on his giant head. "They've got some good players." He gave me a little wink, as if to suggest Kevin might be one of them.

I smiled, but inside I longed for his words to be true.

State champions. The Super Bowl of high school sports. I could barely think the words.

Bud moved up the field, where he stood at the gate, waiting for the team to pour out onto the field. I waved to friends as the stands filled. In a town of 1,300, a Friday night football game is the hot ticket. A coolness nipped the air, spiced with the bouquet of decaying leaves and someone grilling their last steaks of the season.

The band, a motley crew that took up four rows of seats, assembled. I hummed along as they warmed up with the school fight song.

Town grocer Gil Anderson manned the booth behind me and announced the team. I leaped to my feet in a display of disbelief and joy as the Trouts surged out of the school and onto the playing field.

Each player's hand connected with one of Bud's fins on the way to the field.

I spotted Kevin right off, big number 33. He looked enormous with his pads. As he stretched, I noted how lean and strong he'd become over the past six weeks of training. I held my breath as he took the sidelines, wishing for a start for him. To my shock, he took the field after the kickoff, just behind the offensive line.

I've never been one to hold back when it comes to football. I cheered my lungs out, pretty sure the team needed my sideline coaching. And when Kevin got the ball and ran it in for a touchdown, I pounded Gretchen Gilstrap on the shoulders in front of me. "That's my son!"

She gave me a good-natured thumbs-up.

We won the game by two touchdowns and a field goal. As Kevin pulled off his helmet and looked for me in the stands, his blond hair sweaty and plastered to his face, I heard Bud's words again: *"Maybe this will be the year they go to state."*

What is it they always say? Be careful what you wish for?

❄ ❄ ❄

"Amazing run on Friday!"

"I didn't know your son could play football!"

"Kevin has his father's moves—I remember when Mike took them all the way to state!"

I love my church. I stood in the foyer, receiving accolades for birthing such a stupendous athlete, smiling now and again at Kevin, who was closing up shop at the sound board that he ran every Sunday. Mike had already gone to get the car—his favorite "giddyap and out of church" maneuver. I still had more compliments to gather.

After all, Kevin had been a ten-pound baby. I get some credit.

I worked my way to the fellowship hall to pick up my empty pan. With eighty members, sixty attendees on a good Sunday, we took turns hosting the mid-morning coffee break. I had whipped up a batch of my grandmother's almond coffee cake.

Pastor Backlund stood by the door, and when I finally reached him, he grinned widely. "Great game, Marianne."

"Thanks. I'll tell Kevin you said so."

"Must be strange to have your youngest be a senior this year."

I was trying not to think about that, but yes, although I was thrilled to see Kevin move off the sofa and onto the playing field, I was dreading the inevitable quiet that would invade our home next year. I smiled tightly.

"I hope that will leave you more time to get involved at church?" His eyebrow quirked up, as if I'd been somehow delinquent over the past twenty-five years. I was mentally doing the math, summing up just how many years in a row I'd taught Sunday school, when he added, "Would you consider taking on the role of hospitality chairperson?"

"Hey, Mom!" Kevin appeared beside me. "Can I head over to Coach's for lunch? A bunch of guys are getting together to talk about the game."

I glanced at him, back to the pastor. "Sure."

"Perfect," Kevin said, disappearing out the door.

"Wonderful," Pastor Backlund said, reaching for his next parishioner.

Mike, now spotting me, leaned on his horn.

I'd have to call the pastor later and politely decline his offer to let me take command of the weekly coffee break, the quarterly potluck, and most importantly, the annual Christmas Tea. The hospitality position came staffed with women decades older than I, who could teach even Martha Stewart a few things about stretching a budget and creating centerpieces. I'd rather lead a camping trip for two hundred toddlers through a mosquito-infested jungle.

"Be back by supper!" I hollered to Kevin as he slid into his friend's sedan. He didn't even look back.

I climbed into our SUV next to Mike. His thoughts had already moved on, probably to the training he would attend next weekend. Or maybe just to lunch. We rode home in silence. I noticed how the brilliant greens of the poplar trees had turned brown, the maples to red, the oaks to orange. The wind had already stripped some of the trees naked.

I could admit that my leaves had started to turn. But I wasn't ready to shed them yet.

I pressed my lips together and silently begged the winter winds to tarry.

CHAPTER

2

SMALL-TOWN CHARM reaches its zenith when the hometown team has a hot streak. Our Big Lake Trouts had the magic and marched through their season without breaking a sweat, remaining undefeated each week.

Kevin didn't exactly become their top scorer, but he did have two assets that his team counted on: He held the ball as if it had been superglued to his enormous hands. And he went down fighting. In fact, he put his whole heart into the game, 120 percent dedication. Perhaps he had discovered the contagious joy of being a part of something bigger than himself. Perhaps he realized he could move more than his thumbs and still tackle his enemies. Perhaps it was because it was the only thing his brothers couldn't beat him at.

Whatever the case, seeing Kevin work out, study

plays, and drop in an exhausted heap on the sofa after dinner had me beside myself with joy.

I attended every game, regardless of distance. A two-hour trip to Duluth? No problem. An away game on a Saturday morning? I'll bring the rolls. Friday night downpour? What are mothers for?

Secretly, I entertained the idea that I might be their good luck charm.

Team discounts, special menu items down at the Big Lake Café, and decorative slogans painted on store windows or on signs in front yards began appearing all over town. "Rout 'em, Trout!" and "Go, Big T!" I always wondered if the city elders, or whoever had named our team once upon a time, gave any consideration to the difficulty of creating menacing slogans about a bunch of creatures best known for the way they're broiled in onions and butter. But we'd been the Trouts for as long as my memory stretched back—clear to my sophomore year when my father moved us north from the big city of Minneapolis for a slower life.

We took over my uncle's floundering lakeshore resort. Living lakeside soothed the angry teenager inside me who longed for shopping malls and theaters. Meeting Mike Wallace didn't hurt either. Wide shoulders, dark blond hair, blue eyes . . . I met him during the Fishermen's Picnic street dance three weeks before school started and became his biggest fan as he quarterbacked his team through three seasons and finally to the section A state championship.

We'd been together since then, even through my tumultuous years at the University of Minnesota, when I thought I should date other men, especially those pursing an English degree like me. After all, what better pastimes for our old age than lengthy talks about literature? Mike stayed the course, taking his EMT classes, finally becoming a paramedic, waiting for my heart to realize it would be broken without him.

We married a week after I graduated. And promptly moved back to Big Lake.

I occasionally worried about our stretches of silence between football games or church meetings. He'd long ago become the head of our emergency medical services and spent considerable time training new staff, keeping up on new procedures. Our EMS was the best in the county, perhaps in the state.

More often than not, as Kevin began spending more time with his football pals, the loudest noise in the house became the soft rustle of the newspaper as pages turned. Maybe the gurgle of the coffeepot, brewing decaf.

"Are you going to the game this weekend?" Mike asked one morning as I packed Kevin his after-school/before-practice snack of an orange, an energy drink, a ham and cheese sandwich, and a little bag of peanuts.

I reached for the homemade chocolate chip cookies, and Mike raised an eyebrow. "He won't be able to run."

"He needs his energy."

Two cookies wouldn't hurt. I slid them into a plastic bag. "Of course I'm going to the game. It's the division play-offs. They take this and they're on their way to the state tournament." I put the lid on the cooler I'd purchased for Kevin's supplies. "They're playing Lakeside, and since they trounced them earlier in the season, I have a good feeling." I gave him two thumbs up.

He looked at me a long time without words. "Which is why I thought you might want to stay home."

"Now why would I do that?" I tucked the cooler into Kevin's backpack and hollered for him one more time to roust him out of the shower.

"Because, uh, it's your birthday?"

I stopped midstride down the hallway, turned back to look at Mike. "Really?"

"Forty-eight, old girl. I was thinking I'd take you out for dinner." He got up, folded his paper, and came over to me, slipping his arm around my waist. "How about it, Mrs. Wallace? We can even go parking up at Colville Point."

I love the aura of Mike in his uniform—something about the residue of clean cotton mixed with the strength that radiates off him, as if in his capable hands, all will be right with the world. All those years of helping others out of trouble had made him strong and fit, as well as savvy. I hooked my arms around his neck. "But I promised the team I'd give them cookies if they win."

"And she makes amazing cookies, Dad," Kevin said, coming up from his bedroom. He winked as he passed me.

Mike's smile slid just a little. "Yes, she does." But I saw the disappointment in his eyes.

"After the season, for sure," I said, kissing him quickly, then untangling myself to hand Kevin his supplies.

"Did you know it's your mother's birthday this Saturday, Kevin?" Mike asked as he attached his radio to his belt.

Kevin sat in the entryway, sliding his shoes on. "Really? Wow. That's great, Mom. How old will you be?"

"Twenty-three." I glanced at Mike.

"Whatever. See you after practice." Kevin leaned over and kissed me on the cheek. Sweet boy. He'd never caught on that most teenage boys didn't kiss their mothers anymore. I was hoping he'd sail right through without figuring that out.

"Of course. Be careful."

I got the "oh, Mom, don't be such a worrywart" look from my rookie driver.

Mike whooshed out the door behind Kevin.

The cavern of silence that greeted me after they left always rattled me, just for a moment. It wasn't so long ago that Kevin and I would be left behind while the others roared off to school with their dad. We'd read and do laundry and bake cookies together. Kevin was the boy who told me he'd never leave.

Perhaps both of us took that too much to heart.

With October finished and Thanksgiving pressing upon us, I spent the day decorating the house for fall—a straw scarecrow on the door, a couple of stuffed turkeys in the picture window. A brown cloth on the table, with a cornucopia. It would be a quiet holiday. Neil would spend Thanksgiving with his wife, Anya from Califoranya. (He didn't like my rhyme nearly as much as I did.) Brett's new job didn't allow him enough time off to make the trip from Chicago and back, given that we were three hours from the nearest airport. Thankfully, my second son promised to return home for Christmas. Amy e-mailed, of course, nearly every day. I hardly expected her to get on a plane from London for the four-day weekend. Only Brianna would make the trek home from Minneapolis. I kept a stiff upper lip, my eyes fixed on the pinnacle of all holidays—Christmas.

Never had we missed a Christmas under my roof, the entirety of us, and I held my breath in silent dread of the year when one of my five would call with the dark news that they couldn't return home. Even Amy had promised a short jaunt over the pond this year.

I didn't care if they missed my birthday. And I could shrug away Thanksgiving. *But please,* I begged to the silent, gray, snowless heavens as I brought in the giant plastic pumpkin from the front lawn, *send them home for Christmas.*

❄ ❄ ❄

Game day dawned bright, with clear sunny skies and a crisp chill in the air. Kevin declared it perfect and nearly sprang out of bed. I dropped him off at the field, then drove down to the coffee shop for a mocha, a birthday treat. After all, if Mike was going to bring it up, I'd just use that fine excuse to reward myself for forty-eight successful years.

Gretchen Gilstrap was there, chatting with Rachel Backlund, our pastor's wife. They brightened when they spied me, wildly gesturing me over to their table, which overlooked Big Lake. Today the lake looked glassy quiet, the seagulls absent.

"I know this is your first year and all, but I just wanted to assure you that I made a list and put it in your box at church." Gretchen patted the seat beside her even as I stood and stared at her. Gretchen is Big Lake stock clear through to her bones. Her great-grandfather had been the preacher at our church, and her great-great-grandfather, one of the founding fathers of Big Lake. An elegant woman of sixty, especially with her colored tawny brown hair, she wore a wool coat and held a pair of leather gloves. A half-drunk cup of black coffee sat on the table.

"Don't forget it's supposed to be an outreach event," Rachel added. "So you'll need to invite the community." She stirred her chai with a wooden stick, then set it on her napkin, where it soaked through. Her dark brown hair was back in a messy ponytail today, and she looked about fifteen, despite the fact that she had four children, the oldest of whom was already ten.

I sank into a chair, noticing the smallest of ripples on the lake, as if the wind had kicked up. "I'm not sure I know what you're talking about."

"The Christmas Tea. Didn't you agree to be the hospitality chair?" Gretchen had been a key player, if not the ringleader, of the Christmas Tea for roughly a decade. I wasn't sure whose idea it might have been to bring in a new dispensation, but I wasn't eager to be the new queen. I've read the Bible a number of times. Things never go well for the successor of a despot. Not unless their rule is more terrifying than the first.

Were those storm clouds rolling in off the horizon?

"I don't remember agreeing . . . ," I started. And

then, with a whoosh, it came back to me. Sunday morning, a chat with the pastor.

I'd forgotten to call him back, straighten things out. "Oh no. That was a misunderstanding. I can't be hospitality chair—"

"Going to the game, Marianne?" Gil Anderson thumped me on the shoulder as he passed by.

I raised my mocha to him and nodded. "Right behind you, Gil." I slid out of my seat. "I gotta run, but no, I'm not going to be the chairperson."

"But you don't have any kids at home," Rachel said, confusion on her young face. Last I checked, Rachel not only homeschooled her four children, but she also ran the nursery schedule and VBS.

Guilt crept up my throat in a slow stranglehold. "I have Kevin," I squeaked.

Gretchen looked at Rachel, and for a long moment they said nothing. Then, in sync, they laughed.

"Yeah, he's a lot of work!" Rachel said.

She had a point. Today might be his last game, and then what?

"The elders are meeting today to vote you in," Gretchen said. "So you'd better call them."

"I'll do that," I said, already to the door. Hospitality chairperson. I'd rather lie in traffic.

The truth is, I'm not the kind of person who loves to be in charge, to head up big projects. Give me a

broom or a towel, and I'll go to work cleaning the basement of the church after any potluck. However, put me
in charge of a group of women or in front of a crowd
with a mike, and everything inside me turns to glue.

No, I could not—would not—be the hospitality
chairperson.

Outside, a storm had indeed begun to roll in. I
arrived at the school, found my seat in the bleachers,
and waved to Bud, who was suiting up on the sidelines.
I noted he'd brought accoutrements to the game—a
cowbell, a sign, a couple of pom-poms, a blow horn.
I had to give him credit for his enthusiasm.

The team poured out, each player slapping Bud's
fin for luck, and took the field. A fine dusting of snow
had begun to trickle from the sky, landing on the
smooth plastic bench seat beside me, melting quickly.
It accumulated on the field as the first quarter com-
menced.

The Trouts exploded off the kickoff line and ran
the ball back for a touchdown. It would be the only
one of the half. Snow slicked the terrain, turning the
game into a Three Stooges comedy, kids sliding under
each other, hitting the deck without a tackler, dropping
the ball. When Kevin scooted for a few precious yards
through the grip of a defender, it reminded me of those
days when the boys would wage snowball fights in our
backyard.

Halftime was cold and miserable. I scored a hot cocoa from the booster club and found Mike sitting in the cab of his rig. "Happy birthday," he said.

I'd forgotten. Again.

"I'll treat you to McDonald's after the game."

"Big spender," I retorted, laughing.

The Trouts took the field for the second half, and I felt a new spark in the air. They might be cold and wet, and the ball as slippery as the lake in January, but we could all taste victory. If they shut out the Lions, they just might go to the state tournament.

I held my breath.

The Lions received and then drove the ball up the field in a series of successive first downs, right into the end zone. I saw Kevin on the sidelines, pacing. I wasn't sure if he was cold—I had my nose down in my jacket, my hands in my pockets, my hat pulled low—or frustrated.

The team obviously needed my coaching.

"C'mon, Trouts!" My cheer joined Bud's as he went into a frenetic pace of rousing the crowd. He banged his cowbell, waved his "Rout 'em" sign. The crowd roared with his "de-fense, de-fense" chant, aiding the Trouts as they blocked the extra point.

The Trouts failed the next drive and missed the field goal, which only electrified the Lions. They marched down the field again. Thankfully, the fans went berserk, and the Trouts managed to stop them at the one-yard line.

But they couldn't stop the field goal.

The score was nine to six; we needed a touchdown or two field goals to win. I spent the fourth quarter on my feet, losing my voice. Bud, too, had gone all out, dragging a bench to the edge of the field, standing on it, waving his fins, yelling into his bullhorn.

I stopped breathing when Kevin got the ball and ran for a first down, right into enemy territory. *Please, God, let him score.* I wasn't even that greedy for Kevin to be the star—I'd take any player crossing the goal line.

We pushed to the twenty . . . then the ten . . . then the one.

The clock ticked down to less than a minute.

The fans had turned nearly rabid, Bud leading the pack with his fins pounding the sky. "Here we go, Trou-outs; here we go!"

And then, time stopped. I'll never forget how those seconds reeled out, the snow drifting past the lights they'd finally decided to turn on to fight the late afternoon gloom, glittering like ticker tape. The fans exploding around me, the snap of the ball to the quarterback, who then tossed it to . . . Kevin.

A reverse, and Kevin took it around the end. He stepped out of one attempted tackle and stiff-armed another. Dodging a third, he pushed a fourth to the ground and stepped over him.

Go! In my mind he was already in the end zone when a defender crashed into him from behind. I saw the football fly out of his hands—those giant, Velcro hands—and everything inside me froze.

Then, as I stood there, dying, Kevin grabbed it back. He hit the ground with a shuddering thunk, one I felt in my bones.

And the referee's arms went up.

Kevin had broken the plane and landed just over the goal line.

I wanted to weep. Instead, I stood on my seat and cheered wildly as Kevin launched to his feet and was immediately tackled by his entire team. They hoisted him in the air, pulled off their helmets, and pumped their fists.

"Ke-vin, Ke-vin!"

He beamed, wearing on his face an expression of satisfaction I'd never seen before. He'd finally slid out of the shadow of his brothers.

But right behind the cheers, I began to recognize another sound. Something piercing and dark. I tore my gaze away from Kevin and his celebration and searched for Mike.

I spotted him in the ambulance, barreling down the sidelines on the wet track, headed for a crowd of concerned coaching staff who had broken away from the raucous victory.

Beside his bench, his cowbell, his blow horn, sign, and pom-poms, Bud Finlaysen, the team Trout, lay sprawled and unconscious.

CHAPTER

3

THE BIG LAKE MEDICAL CLINIC isn't high-tech. With an ER equipped to stabilize and a small wing for overnight patients, it's more of a triage center. Still, they're the first stop for any Big Laker who needs help, since the closest large hospital is two hours away in Duluth.

Often Mike has brought a victim to the Big Lake clinic and then hours later rushed them, siren screaming, north to Duluth. Or when the situation seems dire, the hospital will call in air support, and the life-flight helicopter will bullet from Minneapolis and land on the pad just north of the clinic.

Tonight I could already hear the blades chopping the air as I peered through the doors of the packed ER waiting room.

Shoes squeaked on the linoleum behind me, and I turned. Mike came toward me, dressed in his navy blue scrubs and a dark blue jacket, the paramedic patch and a number of other certifications dressing his arm. His stethoscope dangled around his neck, and he held each end like suspenders. "Hey."

"How is he?" I had noticed that Marge, Bud's wife, had arrived some time after the ambulance, and a nurse escorted her to the ER. She hadn't returned.

"Not good. He suffered a massive coronary, and if we hadn't had EMS at the field, we might have lost him. As it is, he's in critical condition. They're flying him to the university hospital."

He came close and I filled the rest of the gap, laying my head on his chest. "He was cheering his heart out."

"Literally." Mike sighed and held me a moment, his strong arm over my shoulders. "Good game, though."

I looked up at him, at his smile, remembering Kevin's scrabble toward the end zone. "Amazing game."

"I might be here a while."

"I'll wait."

Mike kissed me on the forehead and returned to the ER, lifting his hand to Coach Grant and a handful of players who'd just arrived. I wondered where the rest of Big Lake had run off to. Yes, we'd secured our position in the run for the state championship, but our entire cheerleading squad had nearly died getting us there.

I collapsed in a vinyl chair.

The last time I paced the Big Lake ER hallways, Kevin had been seven. Always the boy fascinated with machinery and moving parts, he'd been riding his bike on our gravel road when his gaze caught on the spokes of his front wheel, how they whirred and reflected the sunlight. He kept watching that wheel until he steered himself right off the cliff edging the road and clattered into the ditch. Only his helmet saved his life, I am sure, because he tumbled headfirst into the rocks below. Somehow he managed to limp home, where I found him—tear streaked, bloody, and holding his arm. I didn't wait to call Mike, just piled Kevin in the car and drove straight for the Big Lake clinic, where they x-rayed him and pronounced the shoulder dislocated, his collarbone broken.

"What were you doing?" I asked him as they put his arm in a sling and administered pain meds.

"Thinking" was his cryptic reply.

Since then, I'd learned to be worried when Kevin thinks. Not that he wasn't a smart boy—he ranked at the top of his math class. But he had the ability to conjure up harebrained schemes and cajole members of his family into participation. Like the time he decided to spray-paint our dog red, white, and blue for the Big Lake Independence Day parade. Poor Gracie got free and ran through the house, finding refuge in the living room behind the white sofa. Or the time he decided on

shooting practice and attached the target to our basement wall, right next to the sliding-glass door. When
the plate glass pinged, then cracked, and shouting
ensued, the jig was up.

He had accomplices. They all suffered.

Now, as he huddled in a cluster of concern with the
other members of his team, their hair wet from their
showers and dripping onto their sweatshirts, he glanced
up at me. Once . . . twice. The third time I began to
worry.

I knew he was thinking.

I blew into my coffee, got up, and paced away from
his little group of cohorts. The helicopter had landed,
and through the window I spotted the medical staff
emerging from the bay. Mike took the lead, pulling
the gurney transporting Bud covered in blankets. Next
to Bud ran a tech holding a mess of IVs. Someone else
carried portable monitoring equipment.

Marge appeared last, half jogging, half running,
behind them. Despite knowing Bud for nearly thirty
years, I rarely saw his wife. Occasionally I'd spot Marge
at the Ben Franklin, sometimes at the grocery store.
She always looked tired. Rumor said she had a disease,
something that kept her bedridden, yet there she was,
running beside her ill husband. Her dirty parka and
ancient Moon Boots revealed that she hadn't taken any
time to consider her appearance, but I could imagine

myself out there in my ratty blue bathrobe and thread-
bare slippers. She reached out and touched Bud's shoulder right before Mike climbed into the chopper and
loaded him in.

I figured she'd have to stay behind, as most people
with critical patients do. So when Mike emerged and
helped her inside behind her husband, warmth flooded
through me. As EMS director, Mike had probably
twisted a few arms to get Marge on that flight.

They closed the chopper doors, and Mike and his
staff stepped away from the pad as the air ambulance
lifted into the night sky.

I hadn't noticed, but the crowd of boys had moved
in to flank me and now watched as their team mascot
disappeared.

"What did Dad say?" Kevin asked me in a low voice.
He'd cut his hair shortly after the season started, and
it had just grown long enough for it to be messy after
a shower.

"He suffered a major heart attack."

I heard noises of dismay behind me.

"Will Bud be back for next week's game?"

I wasn't sure which heartless teen imbecile had asked
that question, but being the only mother in sight, I
turned and gave them all a look worthy of such a selfish
remark. They cringed.

"We're just worried, Mom. Bud is our good luck

charm. If we can't fin him on the way out to the field . . ."

Fin him? Then I remembered the hand-to-fin high fives the players always shared with Bud on their way out to the field and the worry in Kevin's blue eyes clicked into place.

"We need another mascot."

The words were spoken beside me, but they reverberated in Kevin's expression of gloom.

It took me five full seconds to make the connection between Kevin's previous furtive glances, the words of his teammate, and the dire straits of the Big Lake Trouts.

"No," I said, without clarification.

"Mom, please—"

I couldn't believe it. "Kevin, no. I've spent this entire season packing your lunches, driving to your games, supplying your team with cookies. . . . I'm 100 percent behind you."

"Then—"

I held up my hand. "But I draw the line at posing as a fish. It's just a guy in a costume, Kevin. You can do this without a mascot. It'll all work out." I looked around the group, groping for reinforcements. The team stared back at me as if I'd just told them they had to return a lost puppy to the shelter.

"No," I repeated. I took Kevin's hand. I saw him

blush and knew he was debating pulling it away to save face or letting me have my mom moment, in hopes of enticing me to cave. "Bud's not your good luck charm, because you don't need one. You're perfectly capable of going to state without slapping his fin."

The silence following my words, the deep sighs, and the way Kevin ducked his head told me that they didn't believe that for a millisecond.

"Please, Mom?"

The kid had reduced himself to begging. Right there in front of his friends. And then he put it in overdrive as he pitched his voice low and found my soft spots. "You always say it'll work out, but how do you know? Maybe it's not going to work out at all."

I did say that all the time, but I also meant it. Still, the pleading in his eyes gave me pause.

I saw him suddenly, standing in the play yard, hands outstretched, calling for me. *Mommy, I need you!*

I could feel my resolve give, just a smidge. What could it hurt? It was just a costume—ugly, yes, but something I could sort of hide inside, right?

For one game, maybe I could be a fish.

Then I remembered the googly eyes, the tail. The cowbell and pom-poms. *Oh, please.* I'd rather be the church's hospitality chairperson than humiliate myself in front of the town. I could too easily imagine how the costume would hug my already-ample curves. It would be akin to running naked down Main Street screaming at the top of my lungs, at the height of the holiday season, no less.

"No," I said again, letting that mental image fuel me. "Absolutely not."

Kevin withdrew his hand and turned away. His teammates, clearly embarrassed for both of us, shuffled off. How I longed to offer them a plate of chocolate chip cookies, hear them say, *"You're the best, Mrs. Wallace."* But I couldn't fix this with cookies.

Perhaps it wasn't all going to work out after all.

"Ready to go, honey?" Mike appeared, carrying his radio. He smiled at me, but it dimmed as he glanced at the quiet players. "Marge said she'd call from the hospital," he offered in condolence. I didn't know how to tell him that they were grieving their fish and that I'd dealt the fatal blow.

"Yes, I'm ready," I said, trying not to run from the hospital in a full-out sprint.

The house was lonely and quiet when we arrived home. Mike set his radio on the charger, turned on the police scanner, and went up to change. I didn't mention Kevin's request, not sure who Mike would side with, especially not needing any more guilt.

Fresh as yesterday in my mind was the year I dressed up as Kriss Kringle for Brianna's third-grade Christmas party. And taught Neil's entire fifth-grade class how to play capture the flag during his slumber party. Right behind it, the time I stayed up all night reconstructing Brett's landform sculpture of Peru after the dog ate the bread-dough landscape. I'd even spent a weekend at a Girl Scouts camp with Amy, listening to the giggling of fifteen twelve-year-old girls.

But none of those things included humiliation in front of the entire town.

I hung up my jacket and put my foam finger on the shelf above the coat hooks. The chill of the game had whistled down my spine and invaded my bones. Despite the stopover at the clinic, I still shivered. I filled a teakettle and turned on the stove for hot cocoa.

I passed by my kitchen desk as I grabbed a mug and spied the light for the answering machine blinking. I pressed the Play button.

"Marianne, it's Pastor Backlund. I just wanted to let you know the elders met and confirmed you as the hospitality chair. You can set up your first meeting, but you'll need to meet soon to get the Christmas Tea under way. Thank you for serving! Call me if you have any questions." His cheery voice betrayed no hint of the conversation I'd had with his wife so long ago before the game.

And of course, I'd forgotten to call.

I sank down at the kitchen table, closed my eyes, folded my arms, and rested my head on them. I distinctly remembered saying no, but I could imagine the dismay Pastor Backlund and Gretchen Gilstrap would express if I backed out. It was one thing to decline, yet another to leave the church in the lurch. I kept my commitments. Even when I hadn't really made them.

I wanted to throw the mug across the room, but it was one that I'd gotten from Neil when he went on a missions trip to Kentucky.

Besides, I had possibly found the one thing worse than being the hospitality chairperson. Images of Bud waving his fins on the bench, shiny and glistening under the field lights, slipped through my mind. Perhaps serving my church would be my penance for turning down my son and his needy compatriots. For being a traitor at the height of their need.

I could hear Mike upstairs, humming as he changed out of his uniform. Darkness pressed against the windows. The wind had started to howl, and I hoped a full-out blizzard might be in the making. Maybe we'd get snowed in and they'd call off the rest of the football season.

Then again, we lived in Minnesota. I'm not sure we've ever had a snow day in the history of the county. And this was the run for state.

The water began to heat on the stove, rattling the teakettle.

I wondered if Bud had made it through the flight,

if Marge had anyone with her. The thought of being alone in a hospital if something happened to Mike made me press a hand to my empty stomach.

Certainly I wouldn't be alone. Certainly my children would come to my aid, stand beside me in my darkest hour. Just like I had with them.

Well, at least four of them would.

Headlights in the drive skimmed the naked poplar trees, flashed in our front windows. Kevin had finally inherited the children's car, a little red Honda that probably had about six million miles on it. What it saved on gas mileage it made up for in incidental repairs, but it had taught my children the basics of keeping a vehicle tuned.

I braced myself for Kevin's entrance, pretty sure we'd pick up where we left off. As the youngest, he had learned how to slink away, regroup, and wage a counterattack. However, he came in, dropped his gear, and instead of predictably stomping off to his room as a preamble to his tirade, he detoured toward me, dropping a hand on my shoulder.

"Maybe we don't need a mascot or a lucky charm," he said softly. "Thanks for going to all my games." He leaned over and sweetly kissed my cheek. "Happy birthday, Mom."

Oh, boy. "Thanks, Kev. Good game tonight. Amazing catch."

"Yeah. It's been fun." He gave my shoulder a squeeze. "I'll be downstairs."

Down in his lair.

Down, never to be seen again.

I wasn't ready for the team to give up or for this season to end. Not yet. I needed more victories.

I needed more of the Kevin I'd seen bursting from his shell.

Besides, like I said, I fancied the thought of being his lucky charm. Of course they needed a mascot!

"Kevin," I said softly, my gaze flicking to him. He stopped, turned. In his eyes I saw the boy who had given me a homemade planter in fourth grade for Christmas, working every day after school for a month in the garage. The boy who had once brought home long-stemmed daisies, muddy from where they'd been yanked from the ground. The boy who'd asked me to tuck him into bed until eighth grade.

The young man who'd scored the winning touchdown and taken the Big Lake Trouts to a division championship.

"One game." I held up a finger, just to make sure we were communicating in many different forms. "One game. And then you'll have to find someone else to be the Trout."

A smile broke over his face, one that warmed me

clear through to my chilly bones. The kettle on the stove began to whistle. I ignored it.

"You're the greatest, Mom," he said and held out his hand in a fist. I met it with my own, something I'd learned from watching his pals.

I was a pal.

"I'm calling Coach. He took the suit home from the hospital."

Swell. I got up and turned off the heat on the stove, forgoing the hot cocoa. No need—I was already starting to sweat.

CHAPTER

4

"What do you have against hospitality?"

I was in the kitchen, rinsing off the stew pot, when Mike leaned against the island and posed the question, holding a cup of decaf I'd freshly brewed after supper. I had to admit, after having made not only my mother's award-winning beef stew from scratch but accompanying yeast rolls for dinner, I didn't know what to make of his question.

I placed the pot in the drying rack and wiped my hands on a towel. "I don't have anything against hospitality. I'm a fan of it, to be honest. More hospitality, I say."

"No, I mean the hospitality committee at church. What do you have against leading the committee? I'm pretty sure there is something in the Bible about it being a good thing, entertaining angels and all."

I pulled up a stool. Kevin was downstairs, finishing

up some homework. He'd come home today still buoy-
ant at my Trout concession, and I'd even received a
thank-you from Coach Grant. I hadn't told Mike yet.
In fact, I hadn't told anyone. The truth was, I still
couldn't look myself in the mirror.

I'd caved.

And soon I'd be the laughingstock of the town. I
started to think perhaps this might be a small glimpse
of how the virgin Mary had felt, holding in a secret,
waiting for the town to suggest she'd lost her mind
as well as her morals. Not that I'd had any heavenly
visitors declaring my sacrifice a divine plan, but in my
small way, I hoped to be an example. A servant. Someone who extended her hand—or rather, her fin—for
others.

I sipped my coffee, a raspberry chocolate mix from
the newest gift shop in town. Why aren't those brews
ever as good as they smell?

I put down my cup, making a face. "Let me get this
out into the open. I like hospitality. I think it's a good
thing. I've made coffee cake for after-service fellowship
three times a year for the last fifteen years. I've faith-
fully supplied my tuna casserole to the church potlucks
every quarter. It's just that I don't have any desire to
command a troupe that doesn't need a leader. Gretchen
and her gang have run the Christmas Tea since the early
1900s. It's the same thing every year—Jane plays a few

hymns; we have a reading and then the buffet of Swedish meatballs, lefse, Jell-O salad, bread pudding, and Russian tea cakes. Everyone loves it, and my policy is, if it ain't broke, don't fix it."

"But what if it is broke?" Mike sipped his coffee, looking at me over the rim. "What if God has bigger plans for you, and the tea, this year?"

"Have you and He had a conversation about Gretchen's meatballs?" I stood, grabbed a broom, and started on the floor.

Silence bled into my sweeping.

"What if we have?"

I stopped, looked at Mike, who'd turned away and stared at his reflection in the dark window. A dusting of snow from the roof blew across the porch light as the wind kicked up.

"Okay, I have a confession to make. I thought you needed something to spice up your life, so I . . ." He turned toward me, and his expression mirrored the time he'd backed my car into the trailer, leaving a hefty dent. "I volunteered you for the position."

His words went through me slowly. In nearly thirty years of marriage, Mike had never volunteered me for anything. Not a carpool, not a shift on dispatch, not a teaching position at VBS. Even when he served as an elder in our church, he'd refrained from suggesting anything that might take my time away from our family.

"I'm sorry; I didn't hear you."

Mike set down his coffee. "This stuff is awful. Please don't buy it again."

I took his cup, tossing the contents into the sink. "Repeat yourself."

"I hate the coffee—"

"Very funny."

He sighed. "Okay, I've been watching you. And since the kids left, you seem . . . busy. But not yourself. I know you miss them, and I thought maybe using your incredible ability to get the job done for good in the church would help both you and our congregation. I thought you needed a change."

I hadn't missed his use of the word *incredible*. But I narrowed my eyes at him.

He swallowed. "The thing is, it's not about the fact that you make amazing cookies. Or have always organized this family like a drill sergeant."

"I know you mean that in the nicest of ways."

"It's that maybe God has something in store for you this year. I don't know what it is, but I just . . . well, I wanted to help."

I had no words for that. There were times in our marriage when I didn't understand Mike. Like the time he took up wood carving and made us a homemade headboard. Or constructed a remote-control airplane from scratch, crashing it on its maiden flight. Or even invested in exotic fish, finally filleting them and serving them up with clarified butter. He picks up hobbies like I do new shoes. I had the sudden, wretched sense that perhaps he'd turned his hobby attention toward . . . me.

Hadn't raising five children been enough? What if I wanted to take time off? maybe eat out of a box for a change or, egads, not fix dinner?

A little niggle inside made me wonder if perhaps he might be feeling the same twist of panic over our long stretches of silence.

But signing me up for a new job wasn't the answer. Didn't he know me at all? Couldn't he see that while I could organize my army of offspring, my leadership talents ended there?

For a second I experienced the very mean urge to put his name down for sculpture class at the Community Art Colony.

He'd probably love it.

Dancing! I could sign him up for dancing lessons. . . .

As far as the hospitality committee and the Christmas Tea went . . . "What do you mean by broken? Have you even been to a tea?"

Mike smiled. "No. But I notice you don't attend every year."

"I don't like meatballs."

"I don't think you're the only one."

"What do you mean by that?"

"I just think that maybe you could make this the best Christmas Tea ever."

In the back of my mind, I heard a memory ringing. I swept the dust into a tiny pile as it came to me. *The Best Christmas Pageant Ever*—it was a book I'd read aloud to the children when they were small, about a woman who breaks her leg and the victim who must take over running the pageant. As I recall, it turned out to be a catastrophe.

The comparison didn't bode well for my future. I swept the dust pile into the garbage can. "Well, I haven't heard from God, Mike."

"Have you even considered that He might have a plan for you in this?"

"A plan to saddle me with making coffee cake every Sunday for a year?"

Mike took the broom from me. "Maybe there's more to the word *hospitality* than cooking up potlucks and serving coffee."

I knew, of course, that had to be true. After all, the Bible wouldn't say such things as "Offer hospitality to one another" if it didn't have merit. Eating together had been a common activity for the early church and for every decent church since.

The significance of this eluded me, however,

especially as I called the committee meeting to order the next day at high noon.

Gretchen, Rachel, Muriel Schultz—who was a distant cousin of Gretchen's and the head of the Knitters Club—and fellow hospitality newbie Jenni Simpson, who also led the Mother's Day Out group, had dropped everything to attend our hastily arranged meeting.

According to my wall calendar, I had just over five weeks to pull together our tea. I had started to grasp why the menu had remained unchanged for decades. With the timing of the new committee chairs, the deadline rolled in too quickly for a new chairperson to spice up the event.

That, and the iron fist of Gretchen Gilstrap left no wiggle room. She had everything spelled out, down to seating arrangements, and when she thumped a box down onto the table in front of me as we began the meeting, a chill streaked up my spine.

"I've put it all together in a file box for you, including the recipes, past menus, past prayers, and the array of hymns we use." She took off the lid to reveal hanging files, all colorfully organized. Once upon a time, I'd dreamed of such organization in my home office.

"You should call the newspaper about ten days beforehand—they have the usual copy and just need your go-ahead. And Jane needs the hymn lineup soon so she'll know what to practice. And . . . when you're ready,

I'll bring over the Christmas china. It'll need to be hand-washed, of course, but I'll be there to help you."

Christmas china? I scrolled back through my memories and emerged with nothing. Did we use that every year? My delinquency turned me silent.

Gretchen probably thought I was overwhelmed with joy.

I flipped through the files, not sure what to say, where I fit in, why I'd even been chosen for this. A warm body does not a chairperson make.

And no, I hadn't had a chat with God about it yet. My anger at Mike kept me from acquiescing to the idea that the Almighty might be at work in my life. Shouldn't He talk to me first?

"Can I say something?" Jenni raised her hand.

Yes, you, in the back row, with the nursing baby and size two figure? Just wait until you've had five of those bouncing bundles of joy.

"Of course."

"Well, I was just wondering if maybe we could have something different this year. Like, I don't know . . . how about an Asian theme? maybe Thai food? I just love lettuce wraps."

Gretchen stared at her as if she'd suggested dancing nude through the sanctuary.

I cleared my throat. "I guess it wouldn't hurt—"

"It's a *Swedish* tea," Gretchen said quickly, chasing

her words with a smile I thought would crack her face.

Muriel still hadn't recovered from Jenni's suggestion. She placed her hand palm side down on the table, as if to steady herself.

"I know," Jenni said. At her feet, her three-month-old began to squirm. She picked her up from the carrier and cradled the infant on her shoulder. "It's just that we have meatballs every year and—"

"That's the point, dear," Gretchen interrupted. "That's what makes it so special." She put her hand on the baby's back. "Is she sleeping through the night yet? Mine slept the night through at one month."

Jenni looked up at me. I just sat there wondering where my voice had gone.

"The point is to invite the community, right?" Jenni's voice had lost some of its gusto. "I was thinking that some of the young moms I know might enjoy something different."

"It's a *Swedish* tea," Muriel said, as if just now catching up.

Rachel, who had yet to acknowledge the fact that she and I ever had a conversation about my involvement with the committee, leaned forward. "You know, we need to remember that we need to live in peace with one another. If we pray about this, I know God will provide the right answer."

I stared at her, sure that somewhere in there, she'd spoken truth but unable to get past her fairy-tale smile. From a dark place inside me, I imagined that Rachel had come from some distant land where there was constant singing and laughter and small animals could talk and sew.

Jenni's baby had begun to fuss. "I have to feed her. Do whatever you want. I'll be in charge of day care." She put her child in the carrier, stood, and slung her stylish baby bag over her shoulder. "I just wish we weren't caught in a time warp."

Even I felt the zing of her words as she walked out.

Muriel, still a couple steps behind, stared after her, frowning.

Gretchen crossed her arms over her chest, shaking her head.

"Oh, dear," Rachel said.

Maybe Mike had been right. Maybe there was more to this party than the meatballs.

Like, World War Three.

❄ ❄ ❄

I stopped by the grocery store on the way home and scored a turkey for 99 cents a pound. Although there would be only four—*four!*—of us for Thanksgiving,

I purchased a ten-pounder so we'd have leftovers for a week or so.

As I turned to leave, I picked up another one. This time I went for the twenty-pounder, my mind calculating my Christmas crowd.

Sitting side by side in the cart, the two turkeys seemed a visual metaphor of my life. Abandoned at Thanksgiving. Abundant at Christmas. I quickly filled my list—bread for homemade stuffing, sweet potatoes for pie, golden potatoes to mash, corn for pudding, Jell-O for salad, and cranberries for the turkey.

Just because my entire troupe couldn't make it home for Thanksgiving didn't mean I'd skimp for those who did. Maybe the rewards of their efforts would trickle down to the others. I wasn't above bribery to lure my children home as often as possible.

I checked out and noticed the slate gray sky as I drove home. Although we'd had a light snowfall during the last game, only the barest covering still glazed the ditches and fields. We needed a snowstorm, something to brighten up the gray days, to turn Minnesota into a winter playground.

Our Labradorish mutt, Gracie, met me at the door, her body wriggling with joy. Clearly she had something to tell me as she raced through the house, turned, and barreled back toward me at full speed. I slipped by her at the last second, then set the groceries on the counter.

She came bounding back and I rubbed behind her ears. "What is it, girl?"

She broke away and ran to the living room, barking. I sauntered in behind her.

Draped across the sofa, as if it had trekked in from the lake and decided to take up residence in my living room, lay Bud's Trout costume. All ten feet of glistening, scaly fish body. The head had been propped up on the pillow, the mouth hanging open, the tail unrolled onto my end table over my gold touch-on lamps.

Gracie barked again, as if to say, "Holy smokes, Mom, what did Dad catch now?"

"Very funny, Kevin." He must have come home over the lunch hour at school or, worse, before practice with his buddies, and arranged the sea creature on the sofa. I hated to think just how many people participated.

I walked over to the head. Picked it up. Stared at the eyes. As big as my fists, they stuck out like tennis balls, green and black little slits that looked more monstrous than fishy. I suppose it gave a threatening look to an otherwise helpless creature. Inside, a mesh pocket for Bud's—my—head held the piece in place. I debated trying it on, then put it on a chair instead.

Maybe I should try the suit first.

I picked it up, inspected it. I had thought it was made of something stretchy, but the fabric turned out to be canvas, a grayish material that had been painted to sparkle and shine. It had no zipper, just pulled over one's head. As I stood there, strategizing my attack, a smell hit my nose like a bulldozer. Twenty-plus years of body odor—probably from those days when an orange hunting suit would be too sweltering (which begged the question, what exactly did Bud wear when he didn't wear his hunting suit?)—erupted from the costume. I held it away from myself, eyes watering.

Not in a million, billion years . . . I felt sick and slumped onto the sofa.

"You're the greatest, Mom!"

I heard it over and over in my head to the tune of the pep band and the school song. One game. I had promised Kevin one game.

And he'd remember this forever. Sadly, the entire town probably would too.

I went to the bathroom, grabbed the lilac-scented air freshener, and doused the Trout. It got a full body spray and then a second coat. Twenty minutes later, the suit emanating the cloying scent of floral body odor, I pronounced it wearable.

The sun had begun to slink below the horizon. Mike would be home in an hour, and then I'd have some 'splaining to do. Unless I hid the suit until game day.

My pride heartily endorsed that option.

I would simply try it on quickly, to see if we needed

any adjustments beyond refragrancing the costume, and then tuck it away in the garage, maybe under the lawn chair covers, until Saturday's game.

I decided to go in from the top. I sat on the sofa and began to tuck the body up over mine. However, I hadn't accounted for the miles of canvas material that refused to bend as I attempted to force my feet to the bottom. Not only that, but the neck caught just below my hips, and I realized that I'd have to attack from a different angle. I stretched the costume along the living room floor, then, getting on my hands and knees, wriggled into it, arms upstretched to slide into the fins. I popped my head through the top and rolled onto my side, kicking my feet free. A good foot of material hung past them, but I might be able to pin it up. Or duct tape it. Or sew it with heavy-duty fishing line, suitable for a fifty-pound muskie.

I discovered that the fins had hand holes, access for such useful things as attaching the head. But first, I had to get up.

I rolled to my stomach and, realizing I couldn't move my legs, returned to my side, where I drew up my knees. Sweat had started to break out along my back and the body odor revived.

Somehow, using all the arm strength I possessed, and thankful that I'd beefed them up with the two turkeys I'd hauled home, I pushed myself to my hands and knees. Instead of putting one leg out, I simply straightened my legs, leaving my hands on the floor.

My eyes began to water from the burn in my hamstrings as I reached for the sofa, then the table, and finally worked myself up to a standing position.

I was breathing like a sprinter by the time I got vertical. And I still had yet to move. I pictured Bud's antics on the bench and wondered how he'd had the strength to walk, let alone jump.

No wonder the poor man had a heart attack.

Which reminded me that I needed to send Marge a card.

I pulled up the edge of the costume and found that the cutout legs allowed more movement than I imagined. I decided to take a little gander in the mirror.

I shouldn't have. I stood there in front of the bathroom sink, speechless. What had looked like a sleek lake creature on Bud resembled on me a rumpled, fat wide-mouthed bass who'd eaten one too many worms. Instead of running down my back in an intimidating razor, the dorsal fin wobbled and lurched as if the fish had hit a metal piling hard early in its life. I couldn't even walk right. The costume made me lurch from side to side.

I was a drunk, fat, crippled bass.

Kevin would be horrified.

I had to get out of this costume. And out of town. As quickly as my SUV would carry me.

I heard the mudroom door open, then shut.

Panic rushed over me. I began to wriggle, struggling to pull my arms out of the fins, to push the costume over my head.

Steps down the hallway. *Oh, please, God, if You care about me at all . . .*

I had only one choice. I flopped down on the bathroom floor and began to squirm my way out of the contraption.

"What in the sam hill are you doing?" Mike's voice.

I froze. I couldn't look at him. Really—I couldn't move. The costume had pinned me down with just my nose showing. When I glanced sideways, all I saw was a slice of the toilet. And then Mike's black steel-toe boots.

I felt hands lift me. Set me upright.

I pulled the suit back into place. I couldn't bear to face Mike. And I refused to look in the mirror. I turned my head and looked out the window. It had started to snow. Soft, fluffy flakes that would turn our town to white. I would simply hobble outside and just let it bury me, encased in scales.

"What . . . is . . . this?"

I closed my eyes to Mike's barely audible words.

He sounded like he might be asphyxiating on his own laughter.

"I agreed to . . ." I couldn't say it. Just those three words attested to how far I'd lost my mind.

"Be a fish."

I winced, nodded.

"Have I told you how much I love you recently?"

I still refused to meet his eyes, but he took my chin and turned my face toward his. "I knew something smelled a little fishy when the guys at work told me you were the bravest person they knew. I thought it was because you were married to me."

"Very funny."

He leaned down, as if to kiss me. "Ew, what's that briny smell? Oh, it's freshly caught trout."

"Go away if you can't be nice."

"I think you need me, my little tuna, because I saw you trying to wrestle out of your scales. Someone needs to pry you off the hook."

"Seriously, how long are you going to do this?"

He took my fins and pulled them above my head, working the neckline over me until I slipped out. I shrank down and crawled out of my smelly tomb.

"Remind me to pick up some tartar sauce. I think we're running low."

"You won't be laughing when I cheer them all the

way to the state championship." I stood, gathering my new body into my arms.

"Oh," Mike said, kissing me on the nose as my own words sank in and produced a groan, "I think I'll be laughing long, long after that."

CHAPTER

5

I ADMIT IT—I longed, prayed, pleaded for rain. Or sleet. Or a blizzard the likes of which the county had never seen.

Saturday dawned clear and crisp and even on the warm side. I started to wonder whose side God was on.

Mike at least had pity on me. He had taken the canvas fish out to the garage and, very carefully, so that Bud could regain use of his costume intact someday (we were all still hoping, even though he hadn't yet returned from the hospital), stapled the Trout at the waist, raising the hem about a foot. From a distance, it looked like our Trout had simply added yet another roll of belly fat.

I thought it couldn't get worse—until I tried on the head. I suppose I shouldn't have waited until two hours before the game, but I simply couldn't bear to pull it over my head, to encase myself in the smell and grime of a couple decades of unwashed hair pressing into the mesh. Probably I was being hard on Bud, but I could have made the same assessment about Mike's state of cleanliness on a Friday night. I'm sure bathing wasn't at the top of Bud's list when he prepped for a football game, not with the cowbells and the pom-poms and the signs to create.

I had created my own sign—"Go, Big T!" Coach Grant had delivered Bud's cheering supplies, and I found a couple of cymbals from Amy's old trap set and fitted them with handles.

I kept staring at the Trout head, grimacing.

Mike sat at the kitchen table eating his shredded wheat, hiding a smirk. "This is the perfect day to be a fish. Just do it already. How bad can it look?"

What, in comparison to the body of the fish? I wondered if people might start speculating that I might be expecting. Surprise!

"There's never a perfect day to be a fish," I muttered.

Kevin had left for the team bus early in the morning. I blessed my good fortune that the game was an hour out of town. Maybe people wouldn't come.

"We need to get going soon. Let's try on the head." Mike dropped his bowl into the sink, then stood there in his EMS jacket, hands on his hips, as if he were a representative from the Game and Fish Department.

I reached for the head and, closing one eye and holding my breath, pulled it on. When it dropped onto my shoulders, the weight of the eyes pulled my head forward, shutting the mouth and pitching me into darkness.

"Whoa!" I said, tottering forward. Mike's hands on my shoulders helped right me, yet as I took a step back, the top of the head overcorrected.

Mike grabbed me again as I tilted backward. "I don't think you're going to be able to do this," he said, his first words of doom since he'd discovered me on the bathroom floor. "Can you even see?"

I held the head in place as best I could. The mouth drooped over my eyes, and I had a perfect view of Mike's knees. "How does Bud do this?"

"I think he might wear a baseball hat."

Yes! I remembered seeing that on him at the last game. I felt better all around. "Get me a hat."

Mike's legs disappeared into the mudroom and emerged a moment later with a hat. I heard him adjust the back before he held up the fish's mouth and plunked the cap on my head.

Then there was light. The top of the mouth rested on the brim, and although I could feel the googly eyes bearing down on me, I could see enough to walk.

Mike grinned. "That was a close one."

Foiled again. I pulled off the head and plunked it onto the counter.

Clearly I couldn't escape my fate.

Mike stepped close, his strong hands rubbing my arms. I'd dressed in a thermal shirt and sweatpants, not wanting to dig out Mike's hunting gear and add to the padded effect. "Are you okay?" he asked.

I sighed.

"You can do this, you know."

I nodded. "That's not it."

"You're a good mom."

"I know." I sighed again.

"Then what is it?"

I made a face. "I think you're going to have to help me get dressed."

He laughed and pulled me to himself. "Oh, you cute little trout, you."

We arranged to meet at the game, where he would dress me. I felt like I had when I was pregnant, near the end, and I had to ask him to tie my shoes.

He loaded the Trout into my SUV, and I dropped him off at the EMS station. He didn't have to work today but wanted to check in. He would ride out with some of his EMS pals and meet me at the game.

Which gave me an hour to sit and ponder my life as I drove.

I'd seen Jenni Simpson in the store yesterday, the day after our meeting. She cornered me next to the lunch-meat section. She had her baby in a car seat propped on the shopping cart.

"I just don't understand why we can't have some-thing different for our tea theme. We young moms never get a chance to get out. It's our one chance to dress up, and we have to eat Swedish meatballs?"

I reached for the sliced ham, trying to be a peace-maker. "I know, Jenni. And I appreciate your sugges-tions. I'll talk to Gretchen. It's just that she's put a lot of time—"

"I thought it would be different with you," Jenni said, arms folded. "I thought you would figure out that this tea is for everybody. It's supposed to be an out-reach, something everyone would enjoy going to. Not just Gretchen and her cronies."

"Jenni—"

"Whatever." She threw a package of hot dogs into her cart. "I shouldn't have said anything."

Well, maybe not in those exact words. But they con-tained enough truth around the barbs to stick with me, make me think.

Why, exactly, did we have a Christmas Tea? Was Jenni right? Or did Gretchen and her "cronies" deserve to keep their traditions? After all, they were the back-bone of the church, and most of them watched the babies in Jenni's Mother's Day Out group once a month. That seemed to merit some recognition.

As I pulled up to the stadium, I could taste the excitement. From the band unloading from the bus, to the football players chanting on the field for their warm-ups, to the smell of hot dogs grilling on hibachis, football fever ladened the air.

The Miller Creek Moose would fight the Big Lake Trouts at a mutual location—a meet-in-the-middle city stadium twice the size of ours. Thankfully, we'd drawn home-team status.

I opened the trunk and grabbed the box of my cheering paraphernalia, then trekked toward the field. I waved to one of the offensive line coaches, who opened the gate and let me through to the sidelines.

I had never been on the sidelines, not during a real game. I'd never made the cheerleading squad—not that it mattered to Mike—but I'd always longed to be one of those girls who could jump and touch her toes, climb on each other's shoulders, do a flip in midair.

I didn't even want to think about the way I'd be making my debut cheering performance. I set the box down near the fence and returned to my car.

I noticed Mike standing with the EMS crew from the local county.

He waved to me and pointed to the back of their rig.

Yeah, I remembered.

Pulling the costume out of the trunk, I draped it over my shoulders, grabbed the head, and snuck over to the ambulance.

I went in a human woman. And came out a *Salvelinus namaycush*, according to Mike, who had taken the time to look up the official name for trout in his never-ending quest to mock me. I especially loved the "saliva" part of the name.

Good thing we were married, because Mike pulled and prodded the costume onto me and then had to wrestle me to a standing position. He held the head and popped me a quick kiss before lowering it over my head. "Go get 'em, Trout Girl."

"Rah," I said. But I had to admit, the look of appreciation on his face made me think that perhaps this might be better than being one of those shapely cheerleaders.

No, probably not.

"Wish me luck!"

"Oh, you're the luck, babe!" He patted me on my fishy backside and I waddled my way to the field. With Mike's alterations to the costume, I could actually jog if I wanted to. I might even be able to do a little sideline jig.

A strange power began to fill me as I walked through the crowd. People parted for me. A few gave me a thumbs-up.

I raised my fin. "Go, Trouts!"

I decided to do a little pregame cheering warm-up and stopped in the parking lot, right outside the stands, holding out my fin.

Fans whacked it as they went past.

"Yeah, Trouts!"

Smiles abounded.

"Go get 'em!"

I spied Gretchen Gilstrap approaching, her five- and six-year-old grandchildren in tow. Her eldest grandson played on the team with Kevin. For a second I wasn't sure if I should run, hide, or just pretend like I didn't know her. But she stopped in front of me, a look of confusion on her face. "Marianne?"

"Hello, Gretchen!" I decided that no explanation might be the best, so instead I bent over at the waist, intent on offering her grandson a chance to fin me. "Hey there! Are you a Trout fan?"

He reminded me of Neil, with his pudgy cheeks pressed together in a hat that tied under his chin. His yellow jacket sporting a school bus. His blue eyes peering up at me. I held out my fin.

As I watched, those sweet eyes filled with a sort of horror. He looked at me, looked at my fin, then opened his mouth and screamed.

He shot away from me and behind his grandma, and I think even tried to climb her. On the other side of Gretchen, her five-year-old granddaughter, Amelia, stood paralyzed with terror, not looking at my eyes, but above me. She clutched her grandmother's hand as tears filled her eyes.

"It's okay. It's Mrs. Wallace . . . from church? Remember me? This is just a costume." I tried to open the mouth wider so they could see my face.

Amelia turned and buried her face in Gretchen's jacket.

"I'm . . . I'm sorry," I said, backing away.

"Shh," Gretchen said to Amelia, shooting me a glare. "It's okay. Mrs. Wallace didn't mean to scare you."

As she pulled the still-screaming, crying children away, I stood there, wanting to launch into my own screaming and crying.

I heard chuckling and turned to find Pastor Backlund entering the stands. "It's probably the eyes," he said. "They looked different on Bud."

Yeah, like farther away.

Pastor finned me as he passed. "This is certainly a different kind of ministry tool, Marianne."

My jovial, albeit short-lived, mood sputtered and finally nose-dived into the cold dirt as even Rachel's children carved a wide arc around me.

I gave up and trudged onto the field. Above me, the stands were full of happy fans sitting on their padded seats under their stadium blankets, drinking coffee.

I wondered if I could even see the game from behind the football players.

No wonder Bud needed a bench. I'd need a two-story building.

"And now, introducing the Miller Creek Moose!"

Gil's voice from the announcer's booth registered with me a second before the Moose poured onto the field. Something wasn't right. . . .

And then I remembered: *"If we can't fin him on the way to the field. . . ."*

At the entrance, the Trouts were lining up. All the way across the field.

No. How could I have forgotten?

I calculated the distance and even shot a glance at the announcer. As if reading my mind, Gil caught my eye. He nodded.

I took off around the field, half jogging, half waddling, as if my life depended on it. The game certainly might. Not that I believed in superstition. . . .

Okay, maybe I bought into it a little. After all, if I didn't, I'd hardly be in a Trout suit, would I?

I could hear the stands start to laugh and finally cheer at the top of their lungs. I wasn't sure if it was for me or the team now clustered at the entrance, but I pressed on.

Coach Grant was grinning like a wolf as I stumbled up, breathing hard. "You made it."

"Let's . . . just . . . do . . . this." I held out my fin.

Gil announced our team, and they poured in.

"Thanks, Mrs. Wallace."

"You're the greatest."

"Rock on, Mrs. Wallace."

One by one they finned me.

Kevin ran by. "Love ya, Mom!"

I somehow found my voice. "Go, Trouts!"

Coach Grant and his staff ran last onto the field. I heard Gil on the speaker as I returned to my field position. "Thanks again to Marianne Wallace for stepping in for Bud Finlaysen today."

I looked up and saw that the crowd had taken to its feet, applauding wildly.

Oh.

Mike, who was leaning on the fence near the end zone, caught my eye. He was grinning.

We won the game by two touchdowns. I clanged my cymbals, shook my pom-poms, rang my cowbell, and even made up a fishy dance of my own design. Most of all, I lost my voice and decided that yes, this was the perfect day to be a fish.

CHAPTER

6

IT'S EASY TO BE a celebrity in a small town.

Every week the paper prints the highlights that comprise the latest doings in our community. If there's a fire or a car wreck, of course that makes the front page. In less tragic weeks, articles covering such notable events as the Girl Scouts' holiday bazaar, the winner of the community Halloween costume contest, the annual bake-off winners, and the opening of a new dentist's office keep us Big Lakers abreast of the times.

So it wasn't with great surprise that I discovered a formerly ten-foot, now eight-foot Trout on the front page of the following Wednesday's paper. The picture actually portrayed me in a friendly light—I had cleared the ground and had my hand outstretched in a victory fin five with Coach Grant. And better yet, the angle obscured my face, so those who still wondered who had possessed the body of the Trout were no closer to their answer.

I had survived my stint as a fish.

With Thanksgiving ahead and the next game not until after the holiday, I could push it out of my mind and hope for the best. I'd caught wind of the news that Bud had returned home, and either he would emerge back onto the field fully restored, ready to resume his position as team mascot, or Coach Grant would find a new victim.

At any rate, I hung up my fins and dove into Thanksgiving preparations.

The snow still refused to peel from the sky. I couldn't help but mourn the snowy white holidays when we'd gone sledding or even snowmobiling down our little mountain. I tried to talk Mike into spraying ice on the pond to smooth it out, but he gently reminded me that the last time Brianna and Kevin had ice-skated, they'd both been about twelve. Their skates were probably rusted.

I thought it had been more recent than that.

I washed and ironed tablecloths, changed bed linens, and assembled casseroles. Kevin loved my corn pudding, and Brianna was a sweet potato girl. I baked a pumpkin pie for Kevin and an apple pie for Brianna.

And all this a week before the event.

"You're a little anxious, aren't you?" Mike asked

that evening as he came in. I noticed he had about five copies of the paper under his arm.

"What are those?"

"Keepsakes. The kids need to see this new side to their mother."

"I'm going to burn those when you're not looking."

"Then I'll hide them." He swept past me. "Where's Kevin?"

"Out with a couple teammates," I said, putting the rolls in the oven. He hadn't been home much this week, practicing hard after school and running over plays with his coach at night. I had to admit, I missed the sound of his Xbox down in the basement.

"Amy called. She forgot the time difference and thought it was evening here," I said.

Mike sat down at the table, opening the paper. "How's she doing?"

"Did you know the English have a sort of Thanksgiving Day too? Fourth Thursday in November, just like us. And here I thought America had the market on Thanksgiving."

I pulled out an onion from the fridge and began to cut it. "She sounded so far away. She's dating someone. A Brit." I gave a wry chuckle as my eyes began to burn. "She said it with this cute accent, like she was giving in to the language."

Mike didn't look up from the paper as he spoke. "Remember that time we went on vacation in Tennessee? By the end of the week, you were saying 'y'all.' You and she are like a couple of language chameleons."

Tears fell on my cutting board. "Brett sent me an e-mail today too. Said he was going to Neil's for Thanksgiving, so at least they'll be together."

I slid the onions into the soup pot and wiped my eyes with my sleeve.

Mike's hands on my hips made me jump. "They'll miss a wonderful dinner," he said, kissing my neck. "Although you're going to be so busy on Thanksgiving, it's a good thing you planned ahead."

I wiped the rest of the tears from under my eyes. "No more than usual."

He walked away, and I heard him in the mudroom rustling around as I added the beef, carrots, and potatoes. Kevin loved my stew. I hoped he'd make it home for dinner.

Suddenly, out of the corner of my eye, I saw something lurch into view, dark and silver with green eyes. I shrieked.

"Relax, it's me." Mike looked through the head of the Trout, laughing. "Now you know how little Amelia Gilstrap felt."

I put my hand over my chest. "I thought I left that in the garage."

"I decided to work on it, make sure it fit you right."

"Mike, I'm not going to do any more games." I hoped. Oh, I hoped.

"No, but I got a call today." He pulled the head off and set it on the counter. I turned away from the ugly thing, stirred the soup.

"From Teresa over at the chamber of commerce," he added.

"Oh?" I tasted the soup. It needed salt.

"She wants you to be the Thanksgiving Day Parade marshal."

Me? I turned. "Really? Me? I mean, I know that every year they pick the town's 'outstanding citizen,' but I didn't think they'd—I mean what did I—"

Oh no. Mike had his hand on the Trout head, patting it. Grinning.

"No."

"Yes. The parade committee wants you to wear the Trout."

"Mike—"

"Listen, this is a big year for our town. When was the last time we were in the state championship?"

He knew perfectly well when that had been. I glared the answer back at him.

"This isn't about you. It's about your team. Your beloved Trouts. Think about the players, the coaches—"

"The terrified children! You saw them at the game. They ran from me as if I were the creature from the black lagoon!"

"Which is why I brought the head in. We're going to figure out how to keep this thing from shifting and throwing your eyes around."

Ew. He didn't have to put it like that.

I stared at my husband, at the sweet, teasing smile on his face. Over the past two weeks, we'd had more conversation over this stupid sea creature than we'd had over our beloved children in three years. And I had to admit, I enjoyed his fascination with my Trout costume.

"You're getting way too much fun out of this," I said, putting my hand over his on the Trout. "I guess . . . for the team . . ."

"Oh, great," he said, a look of relief washing over his face. "I already told them yes."

Of course he did. My new personal secretary.

❄ ❄ ❄

Thanksgiving, aka Parade Day, arrived with the slow creep of the sun bleeding into the gray sky. Storm clouds hung low, and a stiff wind took the tarp off our grill.

The thermometer hovered just below freezing, but

the wind chill factor off Big Lake plunged the mercury down to the zero mark.

I gave pride a shove and dug Mike's orange hunting jumpsuit out of storage. Mike wiggled the costume over my girth and then guided my feet into winter boots. My head girded with a wool hat under my baseball cap, I waited until we got to the high school before I put on the Trout head.

Once fully dressed, I lifted my hand/fin to Kevin and his team, who would march from the school to Main Street, right behind me. Our Main Street is roughly three blocks long, so the parade usually went around twice, just to make it worth the while of the folks who'd pried themselves out of their homes to see a few haphazardly decorated pickups with Santa or Frosty on the back. Our church always managed a nice showing, however—a small group of evangelists dressed as Mary and Joseph and the gang handing out candy canes and tracts to all the regulars.

Mike and Kevin had to lift me into position in the bed of Gil Anderson's black Ford F-150. He'd strapped a rope around the cab, something for me to hold on to as he drove. The wind grabbed at my head, and I held it on with one fin as we rolled out of the parking lot toward Main Street.

As we drove, my thoughts split between the turkey I'd stuffed this morning and already set in the oven and the angry cluster of storm clouds. I hoped Brianna had gotten an early start.

Cheers as we approached Main Street grabbed my attention. I had to admit to my poor attendance at the Big Lake Thanksgiving Day Parade in past years, having been much more interested in, say, Macy's. Thus, I was momentarily stymied by the crowd huddled against the wind, clapping their mittens, noses buried in their scarves. It seemed the entire town had turned out to wish our boys good luck in next week's semifinals. And I heralded the pack.

I stood up straight and waved my fin.

Not a child cried. Granted, I was far enough away with my eyes firmly affixed to the top of my head, but still, as I rolled by Amelia Gilstrap and her brother, waving, they actually lifted their hands to wave back.

Or maybe it was to grab the candy the football players threw in my wake. Still, perhaps Mike had been right—this was for my town, my team, my son. A once-in-a-lifetime opportunity.

Halfway through the second swing around the block, the sky let loose and giant fluffy snowflakes drifted down upon the town. I stuck out my tongue to catch the flakes and heard some children laugh. When I looked, they were imitating me.

A Trout of Influence.

Back at the school, Mike helped me down and I slipped, nearly landing on my tail. He wore a grim expression. "The roads south of here are pretty slick. I think I need to stay in town."

"We won't eat until this evening, then. Be careful."

He turned to go. I lunged for him and he gave me a look of concern.

"You have to get me out of this first."

A grin broke through his dark expression.

True to Mike's report, the roads had turned icy, and it took me an hour to get home. I unloaded the Trout onto the lawn furniture in the garage, hoping desperately that Coach Grant would have left a message on the machine, informing me of its next owner. I was starting to get the eerie feeling that such a call wasn't imminent. Bud had returned to Big Lake, but word on the street said he was out for the season. Someone had even mentioned that he needed heart surgery.

The turkey had begun to fragrance the house. I turned on the television and watched *It's a Wonderful Life* as I took out the china, washed it, set the table.

The wind had started to blow the flakes sideways. By the time dusk descended, we had a decent covering of snow on the lawn and piled up against the sliding-glass door to the deck. When I tried calling Brianna on her cell phone, it went over to voice mail.

Outside, I heard a tree crack and looked out the

window just as it fell with a rush to the left of our driveway.

Where was Kevin? He'd mentioned hitting the school gym and then hanging out to run some plays, but I expected him home by now. I stood at the window, a sweater wrapped around me. The house creaked in the wind, and I turned off the television and listened. How many times had I stood in the living room, waiting for Neil or Brett to come home? praying that Amy's date drove carefully, that Brianna didn't have to work too late?

It seemed standard operating procedure to worry. *Please, Lord, watch over my family.*

I called dispatch, and sure enough, Mike was still out helping stranded drivers and attending to a three-car pileup south of Big Lake. I left a message for him.

No one had seen Kevin.

I waged a battle between worry and anger at his insensitivity. It was a draw. I finally took the turkey out of the oven and simply stared at it.

The telephone rang; the noise made me jerk. "Hello?"

"Mom, it's me."

Brianna. I tried to mask my relief, but it flushed out anyway. "Where are you? Are you okay?"

"I'm not going to be able to make it, Mom. I had to retake a test this morning, and by the time I got back to my apartment, the snow had really started to pick up. I keep waiting for it to die down, but the weatherman says we're supposed to get maybe six more inches, and I'm not sure my car will make it. . . ."

I heard more than regret in her voice. I heard fear that she'd let me down, that I wouldn't understand this unavoidable reason why she couldn't come for Thanksgiving. Had I become that needy that my children felt they had to patronize me?

"No, honey. Stay there. In fact, your dad and brother aren't here either—"

"They aren't? You're alone? On Thanksgiving?"

Okay, even as she said it, I realized that I wasn't going to die. I stared out into the darkness, at the occasional whoosh of snow. It was cold out there. I didn't want any of my brood in it, but worse, I'd hate for them to be hurt trying to make me feel better.

Besides, I had Christmas to look forward to.

"I'm fine, honey. You stay put. I'll see you in a month."

Her voice seemed distant and less matter-of-fact than I wanted when she said, "Sure, Mom." We talked for a moment about school and then hung up.

I stared at the turkey, the stuffing, the mashed potatoes and gravy, the corn pudding, and even the pies.

Then I pulled out a knife and some tinfoil and began to carve.

❋ ❋ ❋

The roads had iced over well since my trek home from town only six hours earlier. I had to drive at the speed of molasses, and even then, I saw two cars in the ditch, one of them facing the opposite direction. Both were abandoned. I kept looking for Kevin, but to my great relief, I never saw the red Honda.

I didn't stop at the EMS station or even the school. I had looked up the address in the community phone book and knew the area well enough to know exactly where I needed to go.

I took a right off the highway and headed north, to County Road 53. From there, I hung a left and followed it to Overlook Acres.

I'd only been to the trailer park once in my life, in high school when my mother brought dinner to an ailing member of our church who lived in a tiny mobile home somewhere in this conglomeration of single-wides. Old cars and an occasional snow-covered sofa attired some yards, while well-groomed holiday decorations festooned others. I drove slowly, reading the numbers.

I had nearly given up when I spotted a simple trailer perched back from the complex; it was white and rusty, a rickety porch leading to a door. A doghouse sat covered in snow some feet away, but nothing stirred from the dark opening. I noticed that someone had already shoveled the walk to the porch and wondered if maybe Bud really was up and about. Confirming the house number, I kept the engine running as I got out and opened the back end of the SUV. I'd packed everything in a cardboard box, so I slid it out and somehow managed to not fall and break a hip as I muscled the dinner up the walk.

I couldn't make out a doorbell in the dim light, so I knocked on the door rather awkwardly, holding the box on my hip.

A light flickered on over the porch. A frozen geranium lurched and crumpled in a green snow-filled planter on the rail. Snow drifted across brown plastic furniture.

"Hello? Who's there?"

I wasn't sure what to expect, if Bud could even get up, but I grinned in warm welcome as Marge Finlaysen wrestled with her flimsy metal door. She wore a house robe, the kind that zipped up the front, and no makeup. Her hair stuck up on one side, as if she'd been sleeping.

"Hello, Marge—it's me, Marianne Wallace."

She scoured me with her eyes without a smile. Snow found my bare neck and ran down my spine. I shifted the box into both arms. "How are you tonight?"

She said nothing but gave my box a once-over.

I felt like an interloper on her misery and had the urge to drop the box and run. Instead, I held it out. "I brought you something."

"What is it?" She peered over the edge to the inside.

"Thanksgiving dinner."

Her surprise made both of us offer tentative smiles and then search for someplace else to look. What had ever possessed me to think this might be a good idea?

"For us?"

"Yes. I know you've been taking care of Bud, and I didn't know if you'd had time to get out and shop— so, well, I don't have anyone to eat this, so . . ."

Marge stepped out into the cold now, openly peering inside the box. "You Wallaces have some sort of guilt complex?"

I wasn't sure what she meant by that, but I shook my head. Well, at least none that had anything to do with her.

"Well, thanks," she said, reaching for the box. I unloaded it into her arms. She backed toward the door, which I held open.

"How's Bud?" I asked as she got halfway inside.

"He needs a heart transplant," she said, then looked inside and lowered her voice. "But he only works three-quarter time at the school, so he doesn't have any health insurance. And his Medicaid doesn't kick in until next year." She lifted her shoulder in a half shrug.

"I'm sorry to hear that."

Marge smiled now, a real smile, for the first time. "This smells real good. Thanks for thinking of us."

She was shutting the door when an idea hit me. "Hey, Marge?"

She looked back at me, through the crack in the door. I opened it just a smidge wider. "We have a Christmas Tea at our church every year, and I was wondering if you'd like to come."

Her smile dimmed. "I know about the tea. Every year the church sends someone by to make sure everyone in the park is invited."

Oh. Another task I didn't know had to get done.

"So I'll see you there?"

She lifted the foil on the turkey. Smelled it. My stomach growled, and I hoped the wind covered it up. I had saved some of the turkey, the corn pudding, and the apple pie at home.

"Nah, I never go. It's too fancy for me." She looked up. "Thanks again. I'll tell Bud you stopped by."

I nodded and let the door close.

I was nearly back to my car when the door opened again and Marge stuck her head out. "Hey! Aren't you the fish now?"

I waved my hand. "Yep, that's me. The town's new Trout."

She laughed, warm and genuine, and gave me a little wave back.

I rather enjoyed my new celebrity status.

CHAPTER

7

"WHAT ARE YOU DOING?"

I looked up from the kitchen table, where I had spread out around me three different versions of the Bible, a *Strong's Concordance*, and a Bible dictionary. I resembled a Dallas Theological Seminary student and felt like one after an hour of rooting through the original Greek words for deeper understanding.

"I'm trying to figure out what I'm doing."

Mike shoved his hands into his blue bathrobe, raised a blond eyebrow. "I've been wondering that for years."

"Oh, very funny. I'm trying to figure out the true meaning of hospitality, being that I'm the 'hospitality' chair. Something that Marge Finlaysen said to me . . ."

Outside, the snow still drifted down in gentle fluffs. The spindly birch trees appeared eerily white against the gray pallor of the day. I peered at Mike, grateful that he and Kevin made it home last night and still surprised by their lack of protest about our abbreviated Thanksgiving meal.

For the first time in years, I didn't have leftovers to worry about. China to hand-wash. And I wondered if I had discovered a hidden treasure about Thanksgiving in my snowy night offering to Marge and Bud.

Which had driven me to gather my Bible study supplies and root through the New Testament for references to early church hospitality.

Mike poured himself a cup of coffee.

"Listen to this." I opened my Bible to Romans. "'Share with God's people who are in need. Practice hospitality.'"

Mike sipped his coffee. "See, now this is what I like. No flavor, just good old Folgers."

"It's Sumatra. In my concordance, *hospitality* is translated as 'entertaining strangers.' Like Abraham did when he entertained the angels."

Mike grabbed a roll from the counter and sat down, watching me.

"And in Titus, it says to be hospitable, love what is good, which translates to being fond of guests, and it also implies strangers." I closed my Bible, drummed my fingers on the surface. "I'm starting to think that Jenni's suggestions designed to cater to others are closer to the purpose of the tea, but in the same breath, it's not fair to Gretchen, who's spent years investing in this event. I can't get past the part where we're also supposed to live in peace with one another. What about 'they'll know we are Christians by our love'? If I tell Gretchen and Muriel we're changing the menu, that's certainly not going to speak love to them."

Mike ran his thumb down the handle of his mug. "What is the meaning of love, anyway? Isn't it always looking out for the good of others?"

"My point exactly."

"Except, what would you call the times we had to ground Neil for not finishing his homework or cut Amy off from her million-hour phone calls?"

I got up from my chair and poured a refill of coffee, not liking how much sense he made. "I'm going to make someone upset."

Mike rose. "You'll figure it out, my beloved trout."

I stood in the kitchen, watching the storm sweep snow from drifts and toss it about in wild gusts. Someday—perhaps tomorrow—it would pass, the sun would shine, and the snow would glitter. In the meantime, I would hide myself under a blanket and relish being warm in my home.

Mike changed clothes and disappeared into the garage. An hour later, I heard a motor running. I looked outside to see him camouflaged under a spray of snow as he pushed the snowblower up our long driveway.

Kevin emerged from the basement, hair tousled, and to my surprise, donned his boots and coat and went outside to shovel.

Apparently I was the only one interested in hiding in our snow-covered enclave.

❄ ❄ ❄

Sunday morning, the storm had abated, and we piled into the SUV for church. I saw Gretchen and Muriel in the entryway, having a powwow, and lifted my hand to them, pretending not to see when they gestured me over.

I just wanted to sit in the service and push the tea and the Trout's future from my mind. I sat next to Mike in the pew and closed my eyes, listening to the organ prelude.

I'd forgotten that we had an influential member of the pastoral staff on my committee. Apparently, she'd been dispensing her own opinions around the Thanksgiving table, because when I opened my eyes, perused the bulletin, and saw the sermon title, everything inside me went tight.

The Need for True Hospitality in Our Congregation.
Perfect.

I hung my head through the opening hymn, trying to decide if I should make a break for it. We

Norwegians didn't make waves, however, and I planted myself.

Maybe I'd learn something.

I guess I'd crumpled the bulletin into a tight wad, because just as Pastor Backlund rose to take the pulpit, Mike reached over and eased the bulletin from my hands. He took my hand, his fingers winding through mine.

"As we enter into the Christmas season, it's come to my attention that we may need to explore the meaning of and need for hospitality in our congregation."

I tried to ignore the burn of eyes on my neck. I could just imagine what Gretchen might be thinking.

"Our society is beleaguered with business, people too swamped with their own to-do lists or their family needs to reach past their own front doors and invite people into their lives."

I sighed.

"The problem isn't our inability to provide a decent meal. It's our priorities. When have we looked out past our living room windows to the needs around us?"

I found a smidgen of a smile and began to relax. Maybe Pastor Backlund wasn't talking to me.

"But it's not only about reaching out to our neighbors or our community. It's about our heart attitudes. Do we long to serve others? Do we rejoice in reaching out? Are we loving each other by our actions?"

Mike's hand gave mine a little squeeze. My hand broke out with a slick layer of sweat.

"As we move into this Christmas season, let us contemplate our hearts and whether we should, in fact, offer up first our attitudes and then our homes to serving one another."

I looked down at Mike's thumb and played a game: *1-2-3-4, I declare a thumb war.* My mind wandered to next weekend, when Kevin and Mike and I would search our forest for the best tree, drag it home to decorate. I needed to make sugar cookies and buy cranapple juice to spice up and heat. And I had our Christmas letter to write. I wondered if I should order a fresh wreath for this year.

Mike rose beside me, nearly pulling me to my feet. Phew, it was over, no blood loss. We sang the benediction. I avoided the pastor's eyes as he walked down the center aisle to the back. I'd escape out the side door.

Gretchen must have had my number, because she was standing by my coat in the hallway as I snuck around to retrieve it. "I brought in the boxes of china and left them downstairs to wash. If you need help, just give me a call." She patted me on the arm.

I fought a wave of nastiness.

"Hello, Marianne." Jenni's voice from behind indicated that she'd seen Gretchen. "Did you have a nice Thanksgiving?"

"Wonderful," I said, grabbing my coat. I looked around for a gap in the crowd to evaporate into. "And yours?"

"Perfect. We went to my parents' house. My siblings were all home with their kids."

Of course they were. "That sounds lovely."

"I don't suppose you've picked a menu," she said, all innocent and sweet, the perfect assassin.

"Nope," I said. I patted her baby on the head. "What a cute outfit." Good grief, I was turning into Gretchen.

But it worked, and I made my escape without further incident.

Mike was silent on the drive home. But he was smiling, as if he and Pastor Backlund had collaborated on their recent sermons.

They hadn't, had they?

❄ ❄ ❄

I threw myself into Christmas preparations—spending the week taking down the Thanksgiving decorations; putting up the lights, the wreath, the advent calendars; changing the candles in the bathrooms; hanging bows and ribbons from the curtain rods, the space above my cabinets. I changed the CDs, putting Christmas-only albums in the basket next to the CD player. I pulled out my old Christmas menus. I wrote our Christmas letter, addressed and mailed seventy-two cards, and baked our annual Christmas tree–decorating cookies.

I didn't call the paper.

I didn't wash the china.

Basically, I refused to think about the tea.

And most importantly, Coach Grant never called with a replacement for the Trout.

Pastor Backlund's words niggled at me Saturday morning as Kevin bundled up and left early for the game. "Don't be late, Mom."

Attitude. Attitude.

Mike brought in the costume and laid it on the kitchen table.

Probably I deserved this. Sort of like Jonah, who got swallowed by the big fish.

I didn't particularly appreciate the comparison.

"It's for the kids," Mike said. This time his words didn't come attached to a smirk. He folded one arm around me and pulled me tight. "This too shall pass."

I went down to the basement to grab his orange hunting suit.

Winter had descended upon us in one short week. A glance at the thermometer told me that I'd also need long underwear, wool socks, and probably gloves. I felt like the little boy in *A Christmas Story* who couldn't put his arms down by the time Mike got me dressed in my

Trout gear and out to the car. We drove to the game in silence, me next to my prison guard, sweat ringing my forehead, dribbling down my temple.

I felt like the fatted calf, off to be sacrificed.

The Big Lake Trouts' undefeated record earned them the right to have this semifinal game at home, and the town had turned out in record numbers to support their team. The wind raked the flag over the field, whipping it mercilessly, and a shiver went through me. How I longed to be in the stands, wrapped under a blanket or two, sipping hot cocoa.

Mike helped me out of the car and lowered the head over me. He wore a sympathetic look. "You win the Best Mom Award."

"Just make sure that when I keel over with hypothermia, you're there to warm me up."

That got the faintest hint of a wolfish smile, although I hadn't meant it quite that way. Men.

Please, I prayed to the heavens, despite my theological doubts that God cared who won, *let us win this game . . . quick.*

I could hear the band warming up. The clock on the scoreboard ticked down ten more minutes to the game.

I tried out a few cheers, to which the fans responded. I had remembered my foam finger this time, but when

I put it on, the wind grabbed it and tossed it down the field.

I needed that finger.

I took off, slipping on the snow and ice, my body stiff and uncoordinated. The finger lay quiet in the snow for a tantalizing moment and I lunged for it.

It skittered away from me.

The force of my dive took me off my feet, and with a whump, I fell.

The brim of my hat jammed into my forehead. And I lay prone, facedown.

Maybe I could stay this way.

"Help the Trout!" I heard Gil's voice from the announcer's stand, in between peals of uncontrolled laughter. I couldn't wait to see next week's front page.

Hands rolled me onto my back, and through the mouth slit, I recognized Mike and one of his EMS pals helping me to my feet. "Better stick around," I said without a smile.

Mike had tears rolling down his face as he tried to hide his laughter. He handed me the finger and I grabbed it.

"Help me over to the field entrance," I snapped.

Mike grabbed my arm and we slip-slided to the gate, where I waited for the Trouts' dash onto the field. The opposing team came out first and eyed me with undisguised smirks. Yeah, well. . . . I gave them a fins-down.

The band struck up the school song. While Mike steadied me, I held out my fin and wished my team luck.

Their excited expressions snapped me back to the game, to the fact that we were in the semifinals. One more win would land them, and my son, in the state championship.

A real Christmas bowl game.

"Go, Big T!" I yelled and nearly fell again.

I made it back to the sidelines, grabbed a cowbell, and adopted a no-leaving-the-ground cheering strategy. Mike stayed by the fence as I shimmied my dorsal fin, waggled my googly eyes, shook my pom-poms, and screamed the Trouts to a halftime lead of one touch-down to nothing.

The snow turned the field slushy, and I wondered if Kevin's hands were frostbitten. He'd carried the ball for at least forty yards, at least ten in the touchdown drive.

I sported a thin layer of sweat covering my entire body, thanks to my energetic first half.

I waged a one-Trout halftime show, boogying to the band's renditions of "New York, New York" and "King of the Road," only landing on my backside twice, to the fans' delight.

By the time the team hit the field again, we were

revved and ready to cheer them to victory. The other team—the Trojans, from somewhere out in the iron range—closed the gap with a kickoff return that landed them in Trout territory. They scored a field goal while I led the crowd in a "De-fense!" rally.

The Trouts put no points on the board during the third quarter. When the Trojans recovered a fumble on our twenty-yard line, the stands roared to a frenzy of defensive cheering.

The Trojans connected with their wide receiver in the end zone, pushing them into the lead, ten to seven.

The snow had turned to driving ice. Watching the fans huddling under their blankets in the stands, I gave thanks for the head that protected me from the wind. As I grabbed my blow horn, I took a breath and scanned the crowd.

Bud Finlaysen sat in the front row, way to the left. He was bundled in his orange hunting suit, wearing a wool cap. He met my gaze with something like pride in his eyes.

"Go, Trouts!" I bellowed.

I turned to watch the game for a moment and noticed that number 33 had been added to the kickoff return line. I watched as Kevin knocked over a couple defenders, clearing the road for the ball carrier. What had happened to my timid son?

Or for that matter, to his reserved, cultured mother?

The Trouts took it back to the forty, then over midfield, and finally into field goal range.

Please, don't give in to temptation! Go for the touchdown! But I watched with dismay and a glance at the time clock as they lined up for the attempt.

I turned back to the crowd, banging the cowbell.

They snapped the ball. I could see the play on the faces of my fellow fans. Something wasn't right—or rather had gone wonderfully right! I turned and watched as the kicker—a sophomore with incredible talent—ran the ball into the end zone.

I hit the deck about the same time he did, without, of course, the assistance of a gang of defenders.

"Touchdown!" I screamed, going wild even as I lay on my backside, a flopping fish. But I didn't care. I squirmed on the ground like a ten-year-old, waving my cowbell.

State champs, here we come.

Who was laughing now?

CHAPTER

8

A CONCUSSION AND a broken ankle.

The cost of our superstar kicker's touchdown resounded like a death knell through the corridors of the clinic. Never mind that we were going to play the state finals in the Metrodome in Minneapolis, the same place the Minnesota Vikings played football. Never mind that *this* season, out of thirty, had been the first we'd made it all the way to the state finals.

We had no kicker. Our team barely comprised the requisite number for eleven-man ball, and even then, some of the seniors—including Kevin—played both defense and offense. We had no other kicker.

The dismay on Kevin's face as he emerged from the huddle of doom made me want to wrap him in my arms, kiss him on the top of his head, tell him that Mommy would make it better.

I think we all know by now that I would have marched out in pads and a helmet if it would have been permitted.

"I'm so sorry, Kev." We stood there in silence. Mike was still back in the ER, filling out forms. I had just started to feel my fins, er, fingers again.

"I think I'm going to stick around here for a while," Kevin said, glancing at his teammates.

"What about our tree? This is decorating week-end."

From the expression on his face, I knew he'd forgotten. Hadn't he seen the decorations, smelled the cookies?

"Mom—can you and Dad just do it without me? I really should stay. . . ." He wore that look that said if I forced him, played the Mom card, and perhaps fell to the floor in pleading, he'd somehow find the strength to return home and have fun with us. Merry Christmas.

"Sure, that's okay, Kevin."

He gave me a kiss on the cheek right there in the hall; I counted my blessings and wandered back to the ER.

Mike stood in an equally concerned huddle, only this time it wasn't about the game. "There's a crash out on 61," he said as he saw me approach. "I'm going to have to stick around."

Of course he would.

He waved good-bye and left me alone in his orange hunting suit in the middle of the pastel hallway.

Apparently, Christmas tree decorating was a solitary sport.

I drove home, melancholy pressing into my bones along with the chill.

Three weeks until Christmas. Perhaps I shouldn't be so upset. After all, this was just the warm-up. The real deal happened Christmas Eve, when we frosted cookies, ate soup, gathered for the Christmas story. Mike wouldn't be running out then. Kevin wouldn't forget. The rest of the family would be home to celebrate. I supposed I could even wait to put up the tree then.

I draped the fish costume back on the lawn chairs and traipsed inside. Climbing out of the union suit, I left it nearly fully formed in the entryway.

I stood in the kitchen brewing a hot cup of cocoa, staring at the empty place where the tree usually stands—in the living room next to the stairs, where the ceiling soars two stories. One year we wrestled a fifteen-foot tree into place, its base so wide we had to shorten limbs at the bottom to walk around it. I'm not sure why, but the Wallace family ascribes to a "bigger is better" theme when it comes to Christmas trees. Now, staring at the designated tree spot, I thought of the twinkle lights, the cute ornaments that signified the start of a celebration season.

I couldn't wait until Christmas Eve to put up the tree.

But I also couldn't traipse through the snow to find the appropriate tree by myself. As much as my stint as a Trout had honed my muscles, I didn't have the arm strength to drag the conifer through the woods and set it up alone.

I did, however, have my grandmother's fake tree tucked away in the garage. Once upon a time, I'd set up two trees—one in the living room, the other in the basement entertainment room. As festive as the house felt, the work of decorating two trees had outweighed the joy, and I dispensed with the practice after two years.

I poured all my efforts into decorating our fifteen-foot skyscrapers.

Putting on my boots and a coat, I braved the wind and tromped out to the garage. Some rearranging uncovered the tree box underneath a ripped fire pit tarp, a coil of hose, an old air conditioner unit from our now-defunct camper, and a table umbrella. I kicked it all aside and wrestled the box out, dragging it back to the house. I'd worked up a sweat by the time I pushed it through the mudroom into the kitchen.

Grandma's tree had once been a glorious blue spruce before time flattened its needles and twisted its branches. I spent the next half hour setting it up, pulling out the stems, fluffing it into shape. For being neglected so long, it revived with a Norwegian tenacity, and although it didn't soar past nine feet, the fact that it wouldn't soon be dropping its needles soothed the traditionalist inside me.

Besides, it was a keepsake, in a way.

I returned the empty box to the garage, then found the Christmas lights. It took me an hour to detangle the cords and replace the dead bulbs, a job usually reserved for Mike. Because we had miles of extra twinkle, I wove the lights in and out of the branches, wrapping them with sparkle. The tree could probably illuminate the entire house.

That done, I went downstairs to the storage room and dug out the ornaments. The big box contained seven smaller boxes, all marked with our names. Inside, each child had his or her own collection, one I'd helped create, ornament by ornament, through the years. I put on more water for cocoa and sat on the sofa, opening Neil's box. I pulled out the little ornament of a bear holding a book, the one I gave him the year he'd started to read. I could still hear his little voice, feel his warm body on my lap as he climbed up with a book. We spent hours on the sofa in those early days, just us, and then with Brett cocooned next to me, reading *The Cat in the Hat* or *The Story about Ping* or my personal favorite, *The Biggest Bear*. Under the reading bear figurine,

I found another ornament, a tiny porcelain piano, for the year Neil took piano lessons. I'd spent hours teaching him his scales, simple songs.

I hung Neil's ornaments, poured myself another cup of cocoa, and opened Brett's box. I laughed aloud at the one of Santa on his sled, the little runners of the ornament long broken off. How many times had I found Brett with his ornaments off the tree, arranged on the sofa, coming to life under the magic of his imagination? Almost every one of his ornaments—the beaver with the fishing rod, the marshmallow men with the roasting sticks, the marching nutcracker soldier (for the year we saw *The Nutcracker* in Minneapolis)—had pieces broken off. They took their place on the tree, worn but loved.

Then, of course, Brianna's horse collection. Year after year she begged us for a pony—even drew a map for Santa one year, detailing our house and yard with her suggestions of where the pony could live (conveniently next to my garden). With some melancholy I gave her a different horse ornament every year, wishing it could be a live animal. (*Never,* declared Mike, who'd grown up on a farm.) The Appaloosa, the Arabian, the Clydesdale—the entire corral went on the tree.

Amy's box held ornaments I'd picked up at craft sales—many of them from exotic places around the world brought back by missionaries passing through.

The little Thai girl and the Mexican boy. The Russian matryoshka and the Danish clogs. Amy's heart had been born across the ocean, it seemed, and she'd spent her life longing to travel.

I opened Kevin's box last. He'd been the hardest to buy for, the hardest to understand. The youngest has a way of adopting the traits of those who went before, the hardest time finding his own groove. Inside, the box evidenced his eclectic mix of passions—a miniature figurine of a firefighter the year he had visited the fire station on a school field trip, a dogsled for the years he wore out our *Balto* tape. A soccer ball, for his victory years as a footballer. A miniature Swiss Army knife for the first canoe trip he took with Mike and the boys.

I had purchased a football player for this year—a little snowman with a helmet, pads, and a ball under his arm. I would wait and give it to him to add to the tree.

I finished decorating the tree with my few ornaments and the ones Mike brought into our marriage. I knew I'd hand the kids' personal collections off to them one day, but until they had families of their own, I fully intended to hold these ornaments hostage.

Probably I should have given Neil his . . . and I would—when he came home for Christmas. Maybe I should remind him of that. Or perhaps simply box them up after this season and send them down to Chicago.

Packing up the boxes, I returned the mess downstairs, then sat next to the tree. It had long ago turned dark outside, and the colorful lights glinted off the windows, adding glamour to the room.

I pulled up a blanket, giving the tree a good scrutiny for clumped ornamental groupings. How many years had I rearranged the trees after the children's wild decorating? Now I wished for one of the branches to be dangling low with added weight or one ornament to be hung on another.

In a way, the tree was too beautiful, too perfect.

Lights panned across the windowpane, and relief washed through me as Kevin pulled up. I heard him stomp into the house, pounding his feet on the mat to loosen snow. A few minutes later, he stood at the entry to the living room.

As he was silhouetted in the light from the tree, I couldn't help but notice how he'd filled out, how much he resembled Mike. His broad shoulders had defined with his football workouts, and he no longer carried himself like a child.

Silly, tired tears whisked my eyes. I smiled through them. "How's the team?"

He said nothing for a moment. "The tree is really nice, Mom." He stepped closer, inspecting the ornaments, smiling as some of them helped him capture a memory. He pulled a dolphin off one of the branches, took it in his large hands. "I remember when I got this. It was that year we went to Cancún for Christmas."

Oh yeah, the year Christmas nearly passed us by. Mike, who had to leave the country to get a day off, had concocted a brilliant vacation idea—head to Mexico, where there wouldn't be any icy roads or snow-entombed vehicles, where we could get a tan while the rest of our Minnesota pals waxed pale in the waning sunlight. I'm not sure how he got me to agree, but we spent the holidays in a condo overlooking the surf. Desperate for a tree, I found a palm leaf and set it up on the coffee table. Then, after scouring the shops, I purchased four aquatic creatures fashioned for tourists as ornaments.

Kevin sat down, examining the dolphin, a strange smile on his face. "I think that was my favorite Christmas."

I stared at him, not sure exactly how to take that.

"Remember how we ate mangoes for breakfast that morning? You'd brought along our stockings, and they were filled with swim goggles and suntan lotion. I remember wondering how Santa would find us all the way in Mexico. After that, I never doubted again."

"Yeah, well, that Santa, he's pretty sharp."

Kevin looked at me, warmth in his eyes. "Yes, he is."

He rubbed his thumb along the edge of the dolphin. "Isn't that where you got the clam chowder recipe you serve every year?"

"I got it from the cook at the resort where we stayed. I remember thinking how weird to find a New England soup in Mexico, but you all loved it so much, I decided to bring back our memories and make it the next year for Christmas Eve. Sometimes you just gotta try something new and see if it takes."

Kevin considered me a long moment. "I guess it took. It's my favorite part about Christmas Eve."

The *soup* was his favorite part? I suppose . . . after all, he's a boy.

"I think because it was something different, but also, it was something that made me realize that Christmas isn't just one place and one way, that it could follow us to Mexico or wherever we went." He got up, putting his ornament back on the tree, and stood for a moment with his back to me. "I wasn't at the hospital. I went to Bud's. He needed some wood chopped."

My last conversation with Marge drifted back to me. *"You Wallaces have some sort of a guilt complex?"*

"Were you at the Finlaysens' on Thanksgiving?"

He turned, shoving his hands in his pockets. "I was worried they'd be snowed in and he'd have another heart attack and not be able to get help in time, so

I shoveled their walk." His face turned dark. "Bud has to have a new heart."

"I know," I said softly.

Kevin blew out a breath. "And we don't have a kicker."

"I'm sorry, Kev."

He gave me a small smile. "It'll all work out though, right?"

I pulled the blanket to my chin, stared at the sparkle of lights reflecting against the windows. "Yes, Kevin. I believe it will."

CHAPTER

9

"WE'RE HAVING SOUP?"

The way Gretchen said it, it sounded like I'd suggested having kitten à la king. She looked positively ill, and Muriel matched her expression with a dash of horror thrown in.

"Soup?" Gretchen repeated, for extra whammy.

We sat in the church basement, another hastily called hospitality meeting in progress.

"It's a Wallace family favorite. I promise, it'll be delicious. I found the recipe when our family vacationed in Cancún. It's got potatoes and bacon and clams—"

"Seafood?" This from Jenni, who was rocking her baby with one foot on the car seat. "I hate seafood, and so do a lot of other people."

"We can make two pots, maybe one can just be potato soup, but I promise, you won't even notice the clams—it's delicious."

The dubious looks from my committee told me I hadn't yet sold them.

"C'mon, you've all had clam chowder before, right?"

"I just keep thinking of the cost." Gretchen leaned back, folding her arms over her Christmas patterned vest.

Around us, her beautiful china stacked beautifully in piles told me that she and perhaps Muriel had arrived early to unpack. Admittedly, the ivory china gave a festive aura to our dismal church basement. Festooned with Christmas garland, perhaps a small tree, and Christmas music, the basement could host a simple yet elegant sit-down tea.

Besides, at least I knew how to make the soup, which, after a little sleuthing, I realized was the main job of the hospitality chairperson. After my conversation with Kevin, I couldn't dislodge the idea of serving my tried-and-true recipe to our congregation. Maybe it would be exotic enough to entice others to check it out. Wasn't that the key ingredient of an outreach event?

"It'll be cheaper than Swedish meatballs," I offered. "Which means we can make more, maybe invite more people."

"Which means more babysitters." Jenni pulled out her BlackBerry and scrolled down a list. "I'm running out of people to call."

"The church can only hold a hundred," Muriel offered.

I'd done some research. "We had twenty-three last year. I think we're safe."

Gretchen gave me a look that might have withered a woman who hadn't been a Trout for the past three-plus weeks.

"Do these dishes look like they should have soup served in them?" Gretchen stood and picked up a bowl. The design of holly and wreath, entwined in gold ribbon, ran around the fluted rim.

I kept my voice soft and even. "I wasn't aware that the bowl got to decide what it is used for."

Gretchen opened her mouth slightly. She quickly regrouped. "Have the invitations even gone out yet? or the newspaper been called? It's only two weeks away!" She shook her head. "What have you been doing, Marianne?"

A retort scraped the back of my teeth as I closed my mouth. I glanced at Rachel, who openly displayed fear, and found a smile. "I'm the chairperson, and I think soup is a great idea. I would really appreciate your support and help in this."

Rachel gave a tentative smile.

Gretchen sat down, holding her china bowl. She ran her finger along the edge, slowly. I think I heard a shuddering sigh.

Muriel put her hand on Gretchen's arm.

I felt like I'd called off Christmas. Glancing at Jenni, I saw that she had picked up her baby, rocking her, patting her back. She didn't look at me.

"Please?" I added.

Gretchen put the bowl on the table. "I guess I should start washing."

Muriel got up, and they carried a stack to the kitchen.

I stayed for one stack, but they so neatly ignored me that I decided perhaps they needed a chance to talk behind my back.

Besides, I had some shopping to do.

I stopped by the grocery store, first doing a quick reconnaissance to make sure Jenni hadn't pulled up also (in which case I would have had urgent business at, say, the post office or pharmacy) and priced out the cost of enough potatoes, bacon, onions, celery, and canned clams to feed fifty (why not shoot high?). Then I stopped by the newspaper office to talk to Robyn, who would place our ad.

"Do you want to mention the menu?" she asked as she took down the details.

I debated for a moment. "Maybe just say casual theme and a Wallace family favorite." I smiled conspiratorially. "We're having soup."

Robyn raised an eyebrow as I left. I had a feeling

that by the end of the day most of the town would know that Marianne Wallace had fully lost her mind.

Why stop at being a Trout? Let's upset a century of tradition.

I wrapped my scarf around my mouth and bent against the wind as I hustled back out to my SUV. The lake had frozen over, the harbor one smooth ice-skating rink. In the park, moose-shaped lights fed on snow-covered cedar bushes. Red ribbons curled up our old-fashioned streetlights, and a giant wreath hung on the Welcome to Big Lake sign. Town spirit for the Trouts mingled with the Merry Christmas greetings now appearing on the windows.

"To the dome!" a voice shouted from across the street. Gil Anderson hung out of his truck window, pumping his fist. I raised my hand in greeting.

To the dome! I'd let all the Christmas preparations and the Christmas Tea battle overshadow the fact that in three short days we'd be playing for the state championship.

I needed to snap out of my gloom and get my priorities straight. Make sure the Trout was in good working condition.

When I arrived home, I pulled out my recipe book for the clam chowder. I had a general idea of the ingredients, but I needed to make sure I'd remember everything. I'd forgotten half-and-half.

I was searching the pantry for nutmeg when the phone rang. I scooped it up and set it against my ear. "Hello?"

"Mom—I'm so glad I caught you."

"Neil! How are you?"

"Great. . . . Listen, Mom, I'm sorry to have to tell you this, especially so close to Christmas, but Anya and I aren't going to be able to make it. She wants to go home for the holidays, and since we spent last Christmas with you and Dad, I guess it's her turn."

I closed my mouth, fearing what it might say. Not return home for Christmas? But they hadn't been here for Thanksgiving either. I had half a mind to remind him of the hostage ornaments. Thankfully, my parenting and public relations instincts instinctively took over. "Oh," I said. "Okay. I guess I can understand that."

But I couldn't. Her family didn't even have traditions—I knew, because last year she'd oohed and aahed over our tree, our soup, our Christmas Eve readings. Her family threw frozen pizzas on the table for Christmas Eve, had ham sandwiches for Christmas Day dinner. They didn't even hang stockings!

"We'll miss you," I managed, hating how my voice broke, just a little. "I gotta run—"

"Mom—"

"Really, Neil, that's fine. Have a wonderful holiday. We'll call on Christmas Day."

I hung up fast, fearing he was onto me. I never wanted to be the kind of mother whose children had to cater to her.

Much.

I found the nutmeg, shook it, and decided to add it to my list of ammunition to destroy the Christmas Tea. Then I went down to the laundry room to take out the fresh batch of linens I'd washed.

On the way, I yanked out the Christmas tree lights from the socket. No use wasting electricity on just me.

❄ ❄ ❄

Championship game day arrived partly cloudy, with the sun jockeying for real estate between the clouds. I commiserated, freshly acquainted with how it might feel to be edged out, as I loaded the Trout and my cheering paraphernalia into the SUV in the wee hours of the morning. Kevin and his team had headed down to Minneapolis the night before, staying overnight in a hotel.

"All set?" Mike asked, as he came out of the house. He'd squeezed himself into his letter jacket and wore a Big Lake Trout cap.

I smiled.

He handed me a thermos of coffee. "I'll drive."

The last time I'd been to the dome was the year the Minnesota Twins had grabbed their last World Series

title. Mike had scored us a couple tickets for game six.
I remembered the immensity of the arena, how small I
felt, so insignificant, how the field looked a thousand
miles away. Yet the excitement in the stands soon ener-
gized me, and I experienced the exhilaration of being
a part of something larger than myself, especially in
victory.

Similar to how I felt on a Sunday morning when
worship was overwhelming or the revelation of God's
goodness in my life found my heart anew.

Perhaps that was what celebrating Christmas was
supposed to feel like too.

We landed a parking space across from the dome,
and I used the passes Coach Grant had given me to
walk through the tunnels and onto the field.

The trapped air of the stadium lent an unfamiliar
reverence to the game before us. It seemed our entire
town had made the trek south, yet our population
took up only one small section on the fifty-yard line.
I dropped my gear and my costume—I would suit
up in the hallway—and scanned the opposite side of
the field, easily a couple miles away. I spotted the Forest
City Falcons fans dressed in black and red, clustered in
their group, nearly the same pitiful size as ours.

But hey, we were playing in the dome. I could be
standing right where such greats as Fran Tarkenton,
Carl Eller, and Chuck Foreman once stood.

Except, probably not, since the dome had been built after the reign of the Purple People Eaters.

I jumped up and down on the spongy turf.

"What are you doing?" Mike asked.

"I'll bet you wish they had the dome when you played state."

He gave me a "did you have to?" look. His state championship game had been played at Met Stadium, in a blizzard and freezing drizzle.

"Hey," I said, punching him on the arm, "they made football players tough in those days."

"Please don't." But I saw the smile as he turned away. "I'd better get dressed."

Because we were indoors, I wore only a thin pair of yoga pants and a long-sleeved shirt, thus slipping into the costume easily. I donned my baseball cap and Mike adjusted the head. "I can't believe you get to be the team mascot in the big dome game."

"I know," I said, pulling my fins onto my hands. "It should be Bud in this costume."

Mike gave me a funny look. "I sorta wish it were me."

I gaped at him, unable to speak.

He shrugged. "You always step in and help, and frankly, I should have lowered my pride to be the Trout. And now you get all the fun."

Fun? But I had to admit, despite the humiliation,

being the Trout had made me see myself in a new, um, skin. And allowed me to be a part of Kevin's victory too. I guess I could understand Mike's melancholy. "Well, you can be the Trout's favorite fan."

Mike smiled. "That I am." He held on to the sides of the head, reached in, and gave me a kiss.

We headed out to the field. The Big Lake High band had begun playing our fight song. As Mike climbed into the bleachers, I led them in a wild Trout dance.

Then I jogged to the entrance and stood proudly as our team was announced. They ran through, in clean uniforms, their eyes wide as they finned me for luck.

"Go, Kev!" I said as he ran by me. He flashed me a smile.

While the Falcons poured out next, I ran back to the stands, picked up my cymbals, and roused our fans to a pregame thunder.

Then I turned to watch the kickoff, and my heart lodged in my throat.

Kevin stood at the center, warming up to kick the ball into enemy territory.

When did he become the team's kicker?

Wait! I wanted to yell. What about his Velcro hands, his ability to carry defenders with him as he broke through to a first down? I wanted to see my Kevin carry the ball to another winning touchdown! Not that kickers weren't important, but I wanted Kevin to feel the victory of playing the position he'd worked so hard to master.

He raised his arm, then led the team forward in a rush and kicked the ball.

I heard the fans erupt, but I didn't put much *umph* into my cheering as I watched Kevin assist in the return run tackle, then jog off the field.

I waited for him to return for his stint on defense, but he stayed on the sidelines. Maybe Coach was saving his star for offense. I blew out a breath and picked up the blow horn, leading a round of "Here we go, Trou-outs; here we go."

The line kept the Falcons from a first down, and they punted.

C'mon, Kevin, take the field. I turned, hope bubbling inside me, but there he stood, good ole 33, on the sidelines, eyes on the game.

Disappointment sluiced through me as I clapped my pom-poms together, watching as his replacement tailback got pushed back, time and again.

Kevin would have motored right through those linemen.

I gritted my teeth and picked up the cowbell. I just wouldn't watch the game. I'd simply cheer. But when the fans surged to their feet, I turned just in time to see our QB do a sneak up the middle for a first down.

So maybe they got lucky.

They pushed forward again and landed in Falcon territory. I was eating my frustration when our tailback fumbled the ball. The Falcons picked it up and, fueled by the turnover, marched back up the field and scored.

We ended the first quarter seven points down. To my recollection, we'd never ended a half scoreless, but that's exactly what happened as the Falcons time and again thwarted our offensive line.

Kevin punted four times.

Put the kid in at tailback, I wanted to scream. I seriously entertained the idea of following the team into the locker room to offer some suggestions. After all, I had served as the team mascot for three games and Trout Mother for the regular season. I thought that merited some respect.

Mike must have read my mind, because he came out of the stands and helped lead the halftime gig by starting the wave. I was just about ready to hand him the suit when the Trouts came charging back onto the field. I wanted to catch Kevin's eye, maybe give him one of those "hey, tell the coach to put you in" looks, but he took his place beside the coach as the return kick team went in.

The Trouts ran it back to the ten, where the Falcons held them. "Field goal, field goal!" the fans shouted, all on their own. I was still plugging for the touchdown. Deep inside, I feared that Kevin couldn't get it through the uprights.

They lined up and I waved my foam finger, eyes on Kevin as he took a big breath and signaled for the snap. The placeholder lined the ball up; Kevin took four steps and kicked.

The stands went quiet as the ball soared.

It hit one of the goalposts and careened off. A collective groan went up, and I saw Kevin shake his head. See, I shouldn't have thought those thoughts.

This wasn't fair. Not to the Trouts. Not to Kevin. Not to me. I'd spent the entire season rooting for this team and I deserved to see my kid victorious.

For once, I gave thanks for the giant head that hid my dark expression.

I faked it well through the third quarter, my spirits brightening only slightly when we managed a screen play that allowed Kevin's replacement to slip into the end zone.

Kevin missed the extra point.

Seven to six, Falcons lead, and I was wearing out. The Falcons erupted on the other side of the field, drowning us out. My voice had left me; my muscles ached. I gave a halfhearted clang of my cymbals. "Rah rah ree, hit 'em in the knee!"

I glanced up at Mike, who was finishing the cheer with his section of fans. "Rah rah rass, hit 'em in the other knee!"

He looked at me, gave me a thumbs-up. I didn't

know why he was so cheery. We were losing, and our son was the culprit.

Lord, this was not *how it was supposed to work out.* Furious, I shook my pom-poms. Kevin was supposed to be a star, and me his hero. We were supposed to win this game and have this memory to hold on to forever. It was supposed to be an amazing day, an amazing season, and frankly, I felt betrayed.

After all I did, and . . .

"What is the meaning of love, anyway? Isn't it always looking out for the good of others?" Mike's words, that day when I'd been searching for answers, reeled back to me. *"What would you call the times we had to ground Neil for not finishing his homework or cut Amy off from her million-hour phone calls?"*

What, was this humiliation for my own good? for Kevin's good?

I didn't get it.

A wave of enthusiasm from our fans, the way they took to their feet, made me turn.

The QB had connected with our wide receiver, and we'd gotten the ball all the way to the thirty-yard line. I glanced at the clock. A minute, forty-eight seconds, and four downs to go.

"Go, Trouts!" I jumped on the bench Mike had pulled over during halftime and screamed, doing a trout wiggle.

We edged forward a few yards, then a few more, but the Falcons held us from our first down on the twenty-three-yard line.

There was a lot of space between the line of scrimmage and the goalposts. I glanced at the coach. He was pulling Kevin in close.

No, no, please no.

I shot a look at the clock. Thirty-two seconds and ticking. Enough to go for the first down, maybe even a pass, a Hail Mary into the end zone. *Please!*

But the coach gave my beloved son a little pat on the back and pushed him into the game.

I wanted to slump down on the bench and hold my head or, rather, slink off the field. But I summoned every ounce of proud mother inside me and grabbed my cymbals. "Go, Kevin!

"Okay, God," I said quickly, shooting a look to the fluffy white material of the dome roof. "I'm sorry for my bad attitude. I'm sorry I made this about me. I believe You're up to good in Kevin's life—and in mine too—" the last words came out in a groan—"whatever happens."

The boys lined up to kick. Some fantasyland dreamer inside me was hoping it was a sneak play, that Kevin would run it in for a touchdown, but—

They snapped the ball to the holder.

Kevin took his time, relying on his blockers. Then he took four long steps and kicked.

The ball sailed high, straight. I didn't breathe.

Without wind to derail it or snow to weight it down, it stayed true and sailed like a beautiful gull right through the uprights.

"Yes!" The fans drowned out my screams, but I leaped from the bench.

The team had surged out, hoisting up my Kevin.

I ran straight for the coach. He looked a little shocked when I grabbed him by the shoulders with my fins. "Good job! You did it!"

He grinned at me then. "It was Kevin's idea!" He pumped both hands in the air.

Kevin's idea! I did a trout dance while the coach ran past me and the stands emptied.

State champions.

Mike grabbed me around the waist, lifted me in the air. He wore the foam finger I'd discarded and now pulled off my head and tossed it to the sidelines to kiss me.

"Way to go, champ!" he said.

"Me? I'm just the Trout."

"No," he said, "you're the mom!"

I'm the mom!

I pumped my fist into the air. "I'm. The. *Mom!*"

He laughed.

Our town celebrated on the field as the Trouts fair-gamed the Falcons. News media attended the event, and I saw Kevin giving an interview, as well as Coach Grant and the QB.

Kevin waved to me.

The interviewer turned. Kevin must have told him who I was because he strode toward me, camera and all.

"Can we ask you a few questions?"

An opportunity to brag about my son? Any day! "Sure."

"So, what made you want to be the team Trout? Isn't that taking the soccer mom concept a little over the top?"

I laughed. "It should have been Bud Finlaysen. He's our town Trout. But he had a heart attack three games ago and needs a heart transplant. . . ." I held up my fins. "The show must go on."

"Are you head of the booster club?" He stuck the microphone back in my face as another reporter edged in, listening to my words, taking notes.

"Oh no," I said, laughing. "The only thing I do is run our hospitality committee at church."

This seemed to get a lackluster response, so I added, "We're having a Christmas event, with clam chowder this year." I'm not sure why those words came out of my mouth, but at the time it seemed important.

I'd caught the other reporter's interest. "What church?"

"Big Lake Community Church," I said. "Off of Third Street."

He scribbled it down like he might actually attend.

"Mom!" I heard Kevin's voice behind me and turned away from the press to see Brianna and my football hero running toward me. She had her arm around his waist, grinning, her brown hair cut shorter than I remembered, and she wore a Big Lake sweatshirt and mittens.

"What are you doing here?" I said, wrapping her in a hug.

"I just had to see this Trout thing. And wish my little brother good luck." Her eyes shone. I could see her war between laughter at my appearance and downright pride for Kevin.

Her smile dimmed just a little. "And to tell you that I can't make it to Christmas dinner. I have to finish a project for school that I needed an extension on. It's due the twenty-sixth."

Amid the cheering and screaming around me, I couldn't muster the dismay I knew would come later. "It's okay, honey." I gave her a hug.

She untangled herself and grabbed my fins. "You look pretty good as a fish."

I nodded. Actually, I looked great as a fish. Especially after we'd won the Great Christmas Bowl.

CHAPTER

10

I MADE THE PAPER. Right below the full-page color picture of the team lifting Kevin in celebration. And this photo captured my face and Mike's as he gave me our victory kiss.

I decided this one would be worthy of a frame.

The Trouts paraded back into town, a victory celebration that lasted a week. I rode Gil's truck again in my last appearance as the Big Lake Trout. I waved my fin with exuberance to the team's fans.

My fan was Kevin, who leaped aboard the pickup during the last circle of the block, to wave beside his mother.

My last little minnow.

Back at home, I wasn't sure whether or not to launder the Trout, but I removed the staples and restored it to its previous height, then packed it up along with the cheering accoutrements and returned the lot to Coach Grant's office.

I found him sitting at his desk, looking over rosters. "Already getting ready for next year?" I said, half joking.

"Absolutely. Sure wish your son was sticking around," he added. "He turned out to be the backbone of my team. Almost as if he were captain."

Every mother's cell inside me exploded with pride. "Yes, well, Kevin's an exceptional young man." It was one of the first times I'd said it without a niggle of doubt in the back of my mind. "He's going to go far."

Coach nodded, leaning back in his creaky chair. "It really was his idea to be kicker. I wasn't just saying that."

I hadn't been sure, really. Kevin was never one to volunteer himself for anything, never one to so fully leap outside his comfort zone.

"He said he'd played soccer for years and had been pretty good. I met him at the gym every day for hours of practice. If he hadn't been willing to give up his position for the team, we wouldn't have had a kicker."

And wouldn't have won the game.

"We all learned a lot this season," I said. "So, have you got any prospects for next year's Trout?" I folded my arms and leaned against the doorframe of his office.

"Why? Do you want to give it a go again?"

"Not on your life. My fishy days are over. But it doesn't look good for Bud." Word was that he'd been put on the heart-transplant list, but even if he did find a donor, without insurance, he wouldn't be able to afford the surgery.

"No volunteers so far. But it'll all work out."

I smiled at his words. "Merry Christmas, Coach," I said, turning to leave.

"Hey, good idea about the soup kitchen, by the way," he said. "I've always thought that would be a great thing to do during the holidays, and with the economy, some people are in dire straits."

Soup kitchen? I frowned at him. He met it with one of his own. "The paper mentioned that you were having a soup kitchen at your church next weekend. Even has an address for people to donate to the cause."

It did? I stared at him in horror. "What on earth are you talking about?"

He slid his desk chair back and pulled out his garbage can, riffling around until he pulled out a copy of the newspaper. He opened it to section A, reading a headline on the inside page, next to the religious ads. "'Soup Kitchen at Big Lake Community Church.'" He handed it to me for confirmation.

Sure enough, there it was, not a hint of what I'd told

Robyn when I placed the ad, and every bit a fabrication and potential atomic bomb. "I didn't put out this ad. I mentioned the Christmas Tea, yes, but not a soup kitchen."

Coach shrugged. "I heard a couple people say they were coming."

I looked over the top of the paper. "How many?"

"Ten, maybe?"

Ten? Multiply that by, well, whoever else had read the paper, and . . . I folded it up, stuck it under my arm. "Can I keep this?"

"Have at it, Marianne. Merry Christmas."

I trudged out to my car. Sure, the town's economy had taken a nosedive with the current recession, and more than a couple businesses had closed their doors. Our unemployment rate soared to an all-time high. I agreed with Coach. A soup kitchen could be a great idea.

But it wouldn't stand in the place of the Christmas Tea.

I got into my car and turned on my cell phone. Seven messages bleeped on my screen. Perfect. I dialed Mike, barely keeping my voice pitched at reasonably calm. "Did you read the paper?"

"The rundown of the game? Kevin had three quotes."

"No—the article in the religion section. Apparently

our church is hosting a soup kitchen in place of our Christmas Tea! How could this have happened?"

"Well, don't ask me. I'm not the hospitality chairman."

If I could have, I would have reached through the phone and strangled him. "But you were the one who signed me up."

Silence. Then, "I'll see you at home."

"Don't expect supper. I'll be making *soup!*" I pressed End, wishing I could slam the phone down on something. Add a little resonance to my fury.

How in the world . . . ? And then I remembered my stupid moment of fame. The reporter had asked where the event would be held after I'd opened my big, fat fishy mouth and announced to channel six that we were having soup for our Christmas Tea.

I was an idiot. I wondered if I still had time to book a trip to Cancún. With half my family defecting, it would sure be cheaper. Kevin at least had loved it.

I scrolled through the list of missed calls before listening to my voice mails: Gretchen. Gretchen. Gretchen. Pastor Backlund (or maybe Rachel). Jenni. Gretchen. Gretchen.

Oh, this was going to be fun.

I retrieved the first message and had to appreciate Gretchen's calm tone as she politely asked if perhaps there'd been a misprint in the paper. The calls deteriorated from there. Pastor Backlund mentioned that the church wasn't zoned for commercial use. Jenni wondered how she was supposed to tell her friends that they needed to serve instead of be served when they were already stressed out enough, concluding that she'd probably just skip this year but she'd send her list of potential babysitters to me by e-mail.

Gretchen's final message indicated that by no means was her grandmother's china going to be used to serve a "bunch of riffraff off the street," and if we wanted to do that, then we'd have to add paper products to the budget, which had already been sucked dry by my imported seafood.

Yeah, imported all the way from the canned goods aisle at the grocery store.

By the time I returned home, I just wanted to drink a nice glass of eggnog and listen to Bing Crosby sing "Silver Bells."

The answering machine had come alive with angry red blinking I leaned on the counter, my finger hovering above the Play button. Really, how important was the tea, anyway? Couldn't we save the money and use it for, say, Bibles? maybe supporting a missionary in China? What about buying boots for the needy in Siberia?

I closed my eyes and pushed the button. Gretchen. I deleted it. Backlund, Rachel, who told me that perhaps we needed to rethink the tea. You think? Muriel, who had dialed the wrong number and was looking for Gretchen. Gretchen again.

The last message, however, caught my attention. I listened to it twice before I slumped into a kitchen chair, put my head in my hands, and let fatigue wash over me.

"Mom, it's me, Amy. Oh, I hope you're not asleep and running to get the phone right now. I just can't figure out this time change thing. Hello? Okay, I guess I'll just leave a message. I miscalculated my schedule, and it looks like I might have classes until the twenty-fourth, which means I won't get out until the twenty-fifth and not there until the twenty-sixth, and it's such a long trip home, I'm thinking that maybe I should just stay here. I know we talked about it, and you gave me that extra money to come home, but still—what? . . . Yes, I'll tell her—and Marcus wants me to visit his family, too, so . . . okay, maybe I'll just e-mail you. Love you! Ta-ta, as the Brits say!"

Ta-ta, indeed.

Mike arrived home with flowers. A rare and momentous occasion that only slightly soothed my ragged spirit. I had pieced together a tuna casserole for supper. Kevin, Mike, and I ate it in quiet, me unable to find words for how my life had gone from victory to vanquished in one short day. Mike also stayed silent, afraid of what I might say should he open his big mouth and offer condolences about an event *he* had gotten me into.

Kevin twirled his fork through the noodles, consumed with some dark thought. "I'm worried about Mr. Finlaysen," he finally said. "Me and some of the guys went up there after school, and he couldn't even get out of bed. He looks bad."

I thought of his bad grammar and then of Marge, alone in her old trailer. I didn't know what kind of relationship she and Bud had, but no one should lose her husband over the Christmas holidays. I glanced at Mike as he scooped up the paltry tuna casserole I'd made as if it were a steak dinner. He had become so much a part of my life, my thoughts didn't include one without Mike in it. Long ago I'd dreamed of the day when, with our children out of the house, we'd get to travel or sleep in or just snuggle together on the sofa with full possession of the remote control.

Now it seemed those days were nearly upon us, and the thought of losing him at our prime made the tuna stick in my throat. I gulped it down with some milk.

"Me and some of the guys thought that maybe we'd head up there on Christmas Eve, maybe sing some carols or something."

"Some of the guys and . . . oh, forget it." I knew I was deflecting the issue.

"And then Coach Grant invited us over for Christmas dinner. You know, just us seniors for a little post-game celebration."

I was going to have to kill that man next time I saw him.

I nodded, forcing a smile. "That sounds fun." I breathed a long breath. "I was thinking that I would just call off the tea—or rather the soup kitchen."

Mike looked at me, a worried frown on his face.

Kevin seemed bewildered. "Why?"

"Well, Gretchen Gilstrap and the Knitters are furious that we're going to desecrate their china, and Jenni thinks I've sold her and the other young mothers into slavery. Pastor Backlund is worried about a city fine, and Rachel just wants everyone to get along and live happily ever after." I put down my fork, wiped my mouth. "The thing is, regardless of what we serve, we're supposed to be doing it with a loving attitude. Do you see love anywhere on that list?"

"Rachel wants you to be happy."

"Rachel wants us to live in Gumdrop Land. The fact is, sometimes a little suffering is part of love. According to the Bible, love is sacrifice and serving. And the Christmas Tea—" I added finger quotes to my words—"should be, more than any other event, about exactly that." I tossed my napkin on my plate, then picked it all up to bring to the counter. "I clearly wasn't the one to do this." I meant that as a zinger to Mike, but he was dishing himself another scoop of casserole.

Kevin, however, stared at me, a strange look on his face. "You're going to cancel the Christmas Tea?"

You'd think I'd just suggested selling everything we had to go live in an igloo in Alaska.

"Yes. Life will go on. Did you know that the real meaning of *hospitality* is 'giving comfort to strangers'?" I knew my voice had reached a shrill. "It shouldn't even matter what Gretchen or Jenni wants but what ministers to our community. If we want to have a party for ourselves, then let's just call it that. Not try to make ourselves feel better by saying it's outreach."

Mike had stopped eating, his fork halfway to his mouth.

Kevin put his down. Took a breath. "It'll work out, Mom."

This time, it wasn't a question.

I stared at my son, who had somehow grown up right under my nose. Then I turned away and ran water to send my dinner down the drain.

❊ ❄ ❊

By Sunday I knew I was in trouble. The tea was set for the next Wednesday night, four days before Christmas, and as I walked into church, I felt like the Grinch. No "Merry Christmas" greetings for my ears, no warm hugs. Gretchen shook her head in dismay as I passed by her and slouched down in our family pew, staring at the bulletin.

I signaled to Pastor Backlund as he made his pre-worship service rounds. I could barely speak above my shame. "There's no tea this year," I said.

"What?" He looked at me with concern on his face. I realized, after a moment, that it wasn't a cry of horror, but truly, he couldn't hear me.

"There's no Christmas Tea this year," I said louder.

Of course, that's when the organist chose to end her prelude, leaving my voice to rise into the silence, resound along the rafters, and settle like an executioner's verdict among the congregation.

It spread like wildfire. *No Christmas Tea?*

Pastor's hand landed on my shoulder for a moment and squeezed; then he continued on his way to the pulpit. Mike slipped his arm around my shoulders.

I forced myself to stay in the pew and sing Christmas carols. The moment the sermon ended and the bene-diction was pronounced, I got up. I nearly knocked the pastor off his gait as I ran out of the sanctuary, grabbed my coat, and hightailed it to the car.

Mike joined me moments later. "I think this is some kind of record."

"Just drive."

We were halfway home when Mike leaned over and took my hand. "I feel really awful to have to tell you this, but . . ." He sighed, and something in his tone ESP-ed the message to me.

"Brett's not coming home for Christmas," I guessed.

Mike withdrew his hand. "I'm so glad he talked to you. He called me at work yesterday and told me that his car was in the shop, and he didn't have the money to take a flight and rent a car."

"I'd go get him. . . ." But as I turned and looked out the window, at the now-glassy lake, the snow-topped trees, I realized that I needed to surrender.

No more perfect Christmases. It was over, the season when my children would join me to chop down our tree, decorate it with oohs and aahs. The precious Christmas Eve dinners by candlelight, when we told each other the gifts we'd give to the Baby Jesus. The magic when they'd arise from their beds, surprise in their eyes as they opened their stockings.

Over. I'd had my mom season.

And now, it was just me and my fake tree and a really big turkey.

CHAPTER

11

I WASN'T SURE what to do with my thirty pounds
of potatoes, two pounds of onions, four bags of celery, eight half-gallons of half-and-half, twenty cans of
clams, and four pounds of smoked bacon. Budgeting
my pennies, I'd decided to order it all from a local res-
taurant that offered me a deal, right before the championship game. Perfect timing as usual.

I asked Kevin if he knew of any needy families. I still
hadn't gotten reimbursed from the church for the cost,
so I figured I'd donate it to charity.

Kevin carted it all away without comment.

I kept the smallest amount for our family . . . well,
apparently just for me. Even without my family around
to celebrate, I just couldn't bear the idea of going soup-
less on Christmas Eve.

I had started to wonder if perhaps my traditions
were more for my sake than anyone else's.

I planned on spending Wednesday—the former day of the Christmas Tea—hiding in my home. Kevin had started Christmas break that day but left early anyway, and Mike received a call on his pager about a snow-mobile accident in the woods. The house creaked in the wind, silence filling the rooms with memories as I got up and padded downstairs.

No kids for Christmas. In the three days since Sunday, the truth had sunk into my bones, a dull ache that persisted despite Mike's hugs and occasional jokes about no wrapping-paper mess or kids clamoring for batteries.

I had adult children. Their gifts didn't require batteries anymore. (Besides, I had a veritable military stockpile of batteries in the cupboard, just in case.)

The thermometer had begun to rise over the past two days. Icicles dropped water from my overhanging roof onto the deck, and to my dismay, the snow that dripped from the clouds looked more like rain.

I'm dreaming of a gray, slushy Christmas. . . .

I turned away from the window, poured myself a cup of coffee, and sat on the sofa, staring at our Christmas tree. Gracie settled down at my feet, sighing as only dogs can.

I put my coffee on the end table and noticed my Bible sitting there with the stack of other Bibles and reference materials I'd assembled during my hunt for the meaning of *hospitality*.

With some shame, I realized I hadn't cracked my Bible open in weeks.

I picked it up and thumbed through the pages until I got to Psalms. My marker ribbon opened to Psalm 81, and as my eye scrolled down the page, it stopped on verse ten: "I am the Lord your God, who brought you up out of Egypt. Open wide your mouth and I will fill it."

I couldn't help but think of the Trout. But then I thought of those Israelites and their grumpy obedience. Or often, disobedience. I thought of God's provision despite their bad attitudes—of manna and then victory over their enemies. I glanced at the verse again, almost hearing God say, *"It'll all work out."*

Sure it would. The words now mocked me as I closed my Bible, set it back on the table. Somehow, despite my good intentions, I'd made a mess of everything.

In trying to please everyone, I'd ministered to no one.

As I stared out the window at the drizzle and cold, it occurred to me that perhaps there was one person—or rather two—to whom I could show real hospitality.

I turned up Christmas music as I looked for my clam chowder recipe. I thought I'd taped it to my Christmas Eve dinner list, but it had vanished. I didn't need it, of course, but I thought somehow seeing the smudged little card would bring comfort, tell me that despite the defection of my family, I'd still done good.

I cut up and fried the bacon, onions, and celery together, added the potatoes and water, dropped in the chicken bouillon cubes. I brought it to a boil, let it simmer until the potatoes were soft, then added the clams, the half-and-half, and the nutmeg.

Heating it through, I then covered it to stay warm while I showered and dressed. I dug through my garage for a box and packaged the soup up for delivery.

I added a few other things to the box—some fudge I'd decided to whip up and a dozen gingersnaps that I'd baked last week. I also put in a pair of wool socks I was going to use for a stocking stuffer for Anya and Neil's new scarf. I'd probably overpurchased anyway.

The afternoon sun had sunk into the horizon and bled out through the clouds. I glanced at the clock, wondering how it had gotten so late.

I recalled the directions to the Finlaysens' easily, driving through the mud and crusty snowdrifts to the back lot of the trailer park. I expected lights to gleam through the dingy windows of their mobile home, but aside from a few haphazardly strung Christmas lights, the place was dark.

I sat there in the car, motor running, fearing the worst. Certainly Mike would have called me if Bud had been rushed to the hospital. I didn't know whether to leave the soup or not, so I turned around and headed back to town.

Darkness slunk into the early evening and I turned on my lights. Maybe I'd just stop by Mike's office and see if he knew anything.

The EMS bay was quiet when I pulled up. Odd, since the ambulance stood in the bay, and I knew the ambulance attendants had a five-minute dispatch requirement, which meant they had to be nearby.

I got on the cell phone and called Mike, but it flipped over to voice mail. Kevin's did the same.

I drummed my fingers on the steering wheel, reluctant to return home with my goodies. Not only was I hungry and my loot in danger of being consumed, but our big, empty house in the woods seemed like a tomb to me, albeit a well-decorated tomb.

I sighed and opted to head for the harbor, where the charm of the city lights against the water might cheer me. I put the car into gear. It wasn't until I'd turned left onto the back roads that I realized the route would take me by the dark church. The place of all my failures.

Where was my fish head to hide under?

Two blocks from the church, I spotted cars lined up, people exiting their vehicles. Someone must be having a holiday party.

I slowed, curious as to who might have invited

the entire town, passing the Jamesions' house and the Guenthers', the Thompsons' and the Haydens'. Their houses, aside from the twinkling lights and a few puffy snowmen, remained dark.

I braked for a family of five crossing the street. They waved to me, but I barely noticed.

My gaze had stopped on the church.

Our well-lit, decorated church—the one with the line of people extending out the door, up the sidewalk, around the side, and into our tiny dirt parking lot. I let my foot off the brake and rolled nearer. A large, white, painted sandwich board stood on the sidewalk, outlined in red and green lights, with a flashlight pointed to the words *Soup Kitchen, 6–8 p.m.*

What on earth?

I had to drive two blocks and circle around to the alley behind the church to find a parking spot. I left my goodies in the car and got out, glad that I'd at least showered before I left my house because to a one, every person in line greeted me.

"Hey, Mrs. Wallace, what a great idea!"

"Merry Christmas, Marianne!"

"Community Church has the Christmas spirit!"

I pasted on a smile to cover my bewilderment, excused myself through the line at the door, and wedged my way into the kitchen.

Gretchen Gilstrap stood at the counter, dressed in

an apron, ladle in hand. When she looked at me, we shared a moment of strained, disbelieving silence. Then she smiled. "Wonderful soup recipe, Marianne."

What?

Muriel was beside her, with her own ladle. "It's not fishy at all."

"Hey, Mom!" Kevin, in a white apron, appeared from behind the serving area, carrying a pot of steaming soup in his kitchen-mitted hands. "Comin' through, ladies; comin' through."

I stood back as he poured soup into the kettles Muriel and Gretchen were serving from. As if they'd worked in a cafeteria all their lives, they poured out ladlefuls into paper bowls and handed them to eager hands.

Beyond them, our tiny church basement had filled to nearly maximum capacity. The latest soup recipients moved out of sight.

"Where are they going?" I asked.

"The sanctuary." Pastor Backlund came through and grabbed one of our large garbage cans. "The pews are fuller than I've ever seen on a Sunday." He grinned, though I wasn't so sure he should be excited about that.

Then I heard a voice, laughter that I hadn't heard in months, sweet and teasing. When it ended with "the queen would love it!" I pushed past Gretchen and Muriel and rounded the corner.

There, cutting up celery, was . . . Amy? All the way from London? Dressed in a pink vest and a pair of blue Uggs, as if she had just come in from band practice.

She stopped when she saw me, a smile curling up her face. "Hey, Mom."

The figure at the sink, elbow deep in suds, also turned. "Hi, Mom."

Brett? He looked bigger than I remembered when I saw him last summer, his brown hair longer over his eyes.

"Okay, these are the last of the clams." Brianna came in holding a box. "Howdy, Mom," she said over her shoulder. She had her hair up and looked collegiate in a maroon University of Minnesota sweatshirt.

I opened my mouth, but I couldn't speak. Couldn't move. Couldn't stop the tears from filming my eyes. The room turned fuzzy, and I covered my mouth with my gloved hands. I *had* to be dreaming.

"Hey, Mom. Merry Christmas." Hands pressed my shoulders. I stared at Neil, who looked at me as if he might be surprised to see my shock. Had my son grown old enough to look normal in a dress shirt, rolled up at the cuffs? "Kevin called, said you needed a little help." He pulled me into his arms. For a second, I just stood there, smelling the scent of my eldest son, the one who used to climb into my lap day after day begging for a story.

Anya scooted by me and dumped a load of spoons

into the sink. "I really need this recipe someday, Mom, if I'm going to carry on the Wallace family traditions."

I looked at my brood, cooking, cleaning, bringing in supplies, and shook my head. "Kevin called you all?"

"Not only us, but apparently the entire town or at least your hospitality committee."

"He read us the riot act about hospitality. That it's supposed to be kindness to strangers." Rachel came into the kitchen with her coat on. "Do we have more hot cider?"

Kevin did this? My loafing child Kevin, who, three months ago, couldn't pick up his dirty laundry, couldn't make his bed?

Then again, maybe a clean room wasn't the true meaning of growing up either.

"Merry Christmas, Mom," Amy said as she stopped cutting, came over, and kissed me on the cheek, holding her gloved hands up. "I'm sorry we didn't stop home first. Dad left early this morning to get me and Brett from the airport, and we got here just in time to start cooking. Good thing Kevin took your recipe."

So that's where it went.

"Where do you want these potatoes, Bri?" Kevin came in again, carrying a bowl of freshly peeled and diced potatoes.

He winked at me. "See, I told you it would work out."

I met his eyes. For a moment, we shared a truth that only Kevin and I could understand.

"Open wide your mouth and I will fill it."

With state championships. And clam chowder. And kids who grow up even as you blink.

"Where do you want me?" I said to Brianna.

"I could use some more of those onions cut up, and we need a table cleared out there."

"I'm on it," a voice said, and I saw Jenni, her baby in a front pack, sweep through the kitchen with a tray. She looked at me as she passed. "Someday I need to know all your secrets."

Me too. I rolled up my sleeves and grabbed a couple of cellophane gloves and a knife. "Move over, Amy," I said. "Mom's in the kitchen now."

Brett splashed a layer of bubbles at me, and I waggled my kitchen knife at him.

We cut vegetables and cooked potatoes and added milk and laughed and told stories for the better part of the evening until we finally used up all our ingredients, including the extra potatoes and clams and milk Mike went out and bought.

Beyond us in the fellowship hall and in the sanctuary above, strangers laughed and neighbors reconnected and Big Lake celebrated long past nine o'clock. As the crowd began to thin, I wiped my hands, took off my apron, and wandered into the fellowship hall.

Someone had draped Christmas lights and decorative pine boughs around the room. The haphazard way they were tacked to the molding suggested a teenager's hand. Christmas music played from a boom box in the corner.

White tablecloths, now spotted with clam chowder drippings, blanketed the tables, and in the center of each one . . . a Christmas bowl. Gretchen's beautiful china. And she'd found a good use for the bowls, because in each one, many of them overflowing, were tens and twenties and quite a few hundred-dollar bills.

Someone's hand took mine and Gretchen sidled up beside me. "I think this is what they were meant for," she said softly.

"What's the money for?"

"Didn't you see the sign? We're taking an offering for Bud Finlaysen's new heart. Plus a couple big donors called the church this morning. Apparently your soup kitchen made the evening news last night. There's even a foundation willing to pick up the rest of the cost. It's sort of a miracle, Marianne. Thanks to you."

No, thanks to the Trout and God's sometimes unwelcome nudges.

Gretchen must have read my face because she nodded, a soft look in her eye. "By the way, Bud's upstairs with Marge."

Oh.

I didn't know what to say. I thought about going up to see my fellow Trout, but then I decided against it. He was the real Trout. I'd simply been the stand-in for a short season.

"Thanks, Gretchen," I finally managed, slipping my arm around her shoulders.

She shrugged. "Best Christmas Tea ever."

We cleaned up the kitchen and, to my surprise, even had enough soup left over for the Backlunds, Gretchen, Muriel, Jenni, and the Wallace family to take home. Before we left, Mike slipped my cardboard box into Bud's car. They were probably sick of soup, but perhaps not the other goodies.

As we exited the church, I noticed that the weather had again turned nippy. My breath spiraled into the air as I slipped my hand through Mike's arm. Beside me walked Amy and Bri. Neil and Anya got into their car to follow us home. Kevin's and Brett's voices rose in argument over who should drive the red clunker home.

Above, the sky had cleared, a thousand lights winking down at me, a Christmas card from God.

Merry Christmas, Marianne Wallace.

EPILOGUE

"WHAT A GREAT STORY!" Marci blows on her cocoa, takes a sip, and gets off the bench. She walks over to the cutting board, where I've chopped up celery. The bacon is already browning, the potatoes boiling in the pot. "Is this it?"

I glance at Kevin, and he is grinning at me. "Yep."

"I can't wait to taste it." She sits back down, snuggling against Kevin. "So, did everyone stay for Christmas?"

I lean against the counter. "Amy did, and so did Brianna and Brett, but Neil and Anya headed to her house in California. They do every other Christmas here. But Brett and Cathy come nearly every year. Her mother sometimes joins them."

"Is Brianna coming home for Christmas this year? I know she's busy with her practice."

"Not this year," I say without any sadness. "We'll probably stop by and see her, though."

"I suppose it's hard for Amy to get home. She's almost done with her doctorate?"

"Yes, although she's talking about learning German. Marcus's grandparents live in Germany, and they might move there, although I have a feeling she's wanting to have a baby."

Something twinkles in Marci's eyes. "I can't wait until Kevin and I have kids. To be a mom, wake up in the morning to little feet. I'll bet Kevin was an adorable baby."

I turn away to finish chopping the onions. "They all were."

They still are.

"Did you love being a mom? Was it everything you dreamed of? Would you do it again?"

Would I do the chaos, the late night feedings, the challenges and worries? Would I do the book reports and the piles of laundry and the illnesses? Would I let them take over my heart so that when they grew up and left home, it created this hollow space that seemed cavernous?

But a space that is just the right size for grandchildren.

I turn and toss Kevin a towel. "I need a dishwasher."

"I'm on it." He gives my shoulders a squeeze as he walks by.

I slide the onions into the pot, wipe my eyes, and look at Marci. She's watching me, as if seriously waiting for my reply. "I would do it over and over and over, Marci."

Marci nods, slips her gaze to Kevin, and takes a sip of cocoa. "Oh," she says, putting down the mug. "What happened to Bud?"

"He had his heart transplant," Kevin says. "With what the community raised, as well as a couple big donations, it covered his hospital bills. The church recently helped them buy a new house closer to town. He took over as the Trout again, although I don't think he's quite as energetic."

"We're going to have to find a new Trout one of these days."

Kevin glances at me, waggles his eyebrows.

"Nope," I say. Unless of course Kevin returns home and takes over coaching the Trouts. . . . No! Not even then.

"Does the Community Church still have the Christmas Tea?" Marci asks.

I laugh.

"Not anymore," Kevin says. "Now it's a soup kitchen. Except they call it the Annual Christmas Bowl." He looks at me, back to Marci. "Hey, wanna see my mom's picture as a fish?"

"Kevin, no!"

But he's wiping his hands and thundering down to his room, which remains largely untouched and filled with old copies of the town paper.

Marci leans against the counter, lowering her voice. "If no one is coming home, what are you and Mr. Wallace doing for Christmas?"

I smile, seeing Mike's headlights appear in the driveway. "Oh, we're going to Cancún."

WARREN FAMILY CHRISTMAS CLAM CHOWDER

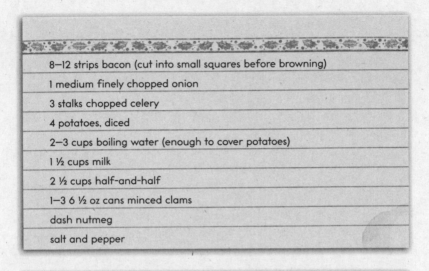

8–12 strips bacon (cut into small squares before browning)

1 medium finely chopped onion

3 stalks chopped celery

4 potatoes, diced

2–3 cups boiling water (enough to cover potatoes)

1 ½ cups milk

2 ½ cups half-and-half

1–3 6 ½ oz cans minced clams

dash nutmeg

salt and pepper

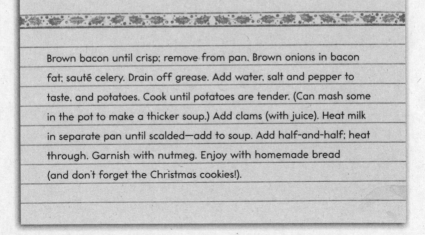

Brown bacon until crisp; remove from pan. Brown onions in bacon fat; sauté celery. Drain off grease. Add water, salt and pepper to taste, and potatoes. Cook until potatoes are tender. (Can mash some in the pot to make a thicker soup.) Add clams (with juice). Heat milk in separate pan until scalded—add to soup. Add half-and-half; heat through. Garnish with nutmeg. Enjoy with homemade bread (and don't forget the Christmas cookies!).

ABOUT THE AUTHOR

SUSAN MAY WARREN is a former missionary to Russia, the mother of four children, and the wife of a guy who wooed her onto the back of his motorcycle for the adventure of a lifetime. The award-winning author of over twenty books, Susan loves to write and teach writing. She speaks at women's events around the country about God's amazing grace in our lives. Susan is active in her church and small community and makes her home on the north shore of Minnesota, where her husband runs a hotel.

Visit her Web site at **www.susanmaywarren.com.**

More great fiction from

SUSAN MAY WARREN

THE NOBLE LEGACY SERIES

After their father dies, three siblings reunite on the family ranch to try to preserve the Noble legacy. If only family secrets—and unsuspected enemies—didn't threaten to destroy everything they've worked so hard to build.